MW01147884

Any references to historical events, real people or real
places are used factiously. Names, characters, and places
are products of the authors imagination.

Front Cover Image by Tina Louise

First Printing Edition 2019

Acknowledgements

First, I want to thank God for being better to me, then I have been to myself. Without HIM, I am nothing. He has given me strength when I was weak, peace in the middle of my storms, vision when I was lost, and hope when I felt like I couldn't go on. His Grace and Mercy Is Everlasting.

To my Father and Mother, My Guardian Angels! Every day without you here on earth with me is hard. I Thank You for all the sacrifices you made for me, that molded me into the woman I am today. I Thank You for all the wisdom, morals and structure you instilled in me. Even when you thought I wasn't listening, I WAS LISTENING! Not one day goes by that I don't thank God for giving me two of the best parents in the world. You were supposed to be here to see this, but I know you are here with me in spirit. I love you and I pray I am making you proud. Keep watching over me and your grandbabies.

To my children my hearts, my loves, you are my daily inspiration. When I have thought of giving up, I had to remember who was watching, YOU! I have made some mistakes in front of you, I pray it has taught you, to let your mistakes BUILD YOU, not BREAK YOU! Your love and loyalty have gotten me through some of my worst days. I thank you for sitting on that Front Row EVERY LAST one of my court dates, I Thank You for being the first face I saw out of surgery from being shot. If nobody Got Me, I know my Kids DO! I could not have asked God to bless me with better kids.

To My Daughter India. You inspire my heart. You have taught me to chase your dreams and never give up. I am OVER proud of the woman you are growing into daily.

A Special Thank You to My Godson/Technology Wiz Dandre. Words can't express how much your computer expertise blessed me throughout this process.

Special Thank You My Daughter Lea Haislip AKA Akeelah the Bee LOL for Editing My Work and Catching All My Mistakes

To My Brothers! Thank You for being some of the REAL ONES left. Last of a Dying Breed!

To My Best Friends, Brandy, Kerry, Valencia, and My Sisters Felica and Porscha. I Thank You for always being my listening ear and never judging me. I thank you for your brutal, unfiltered, no sugar coating, honesty (I Think, lol). You have never held back telling me what I needed to hear, instead of what I wanted to hear. Every woman needs a supportive circle. I Thank God for mine.

To all my supporters, Thank You! Thank You! Thank YOU! I Love You! Without You There Is No me.

To EVERY Woman reading this. If it's ONE message I hope this book sends to each and every last one of you is, No matter how bad your situation looks, NEVER GIVE UP.GOD IS ALWAYS IN CONTROL! The Devil comes to Kill, Steal and Destroy! He will do everything in his power to Kill your Joy, Steal your Peace and Destroy your Hope. You will be Tested, Whatever you do DON'T FOLD!

To all my haters, betrayers and everyone who counted me out. I guess no one told you, I was a seed, every piece of dirt you threw on me, I used to help me grow. I thank you for all the lies, ridicule and efforts used in hopes of ruining me. It made me stronger, wiser and richer!

True Glory Publications and Shameek Speight, Thank You for Providing me with this opportunity. I promise I won't let you down!

If I have Encouraged or Inspired just ONE WOMAN, It Was All Worth It!

Secret Enemy

~One Fake Friend Can Do More Damage Than A
Thousand Enemies! ~

Synopsis

King is a powerful man who has taken over the streets of Detroit. After dealing with nothing but hoodrats, thots and gold diggers, it is love at first sight when he meets the beautiful, sexy and independent Mya Jones. Love will bring them together but will jealousy, lies, ulterior motives and secrets tear them apart.

Mya's life was a dream come true. She had a husband who loved and adored her, a successful career and a best friend who she shared an unbreakable bond with, or so she thought. Mya will soon learn, you may think you know a person, only to discover you never really knew them at all.

Star is the definition of keep your friends close, and your enemy even closer! From a young age, Star has always used her exotic looks and the power of what was between her legs, to make men fulfill her every heart desire, all expect one, giving her the title as "wife". Will Star commit the ultimate act of betrayal to finally get what she wants?

When secrets are revealed and lies are exposed, friends will turn into enemies and leave everyone wondering, if there really is a such thing as a "friend"?

Prologue

After a long day, King wanted to do nothing more than go home and climb into bed. He decided to fix himself a sandwich and watch a little ESPN while he ate. After eating, King stripped down to his boxers and jumped into bed, pulling the covers fully over his head. He would deal with everything going on tomorrow, right now he just needed a good night of sleep. The sudden feel of heavy pressure on his chest awoke King from his sleep. His eyes popped wide open at the sight of his wife, straddled across his body, holding a gun to the middle of his forehand. Baby Wait!", King screamed. He tried not to make any sudden moves to startle his wife and cause her to accidently pull the trigger on the gun she was holding to the middle of his forehead. "I trusted you!", Mya sobbed, lightly brushing the tip of the gun against King's face. King could see the hurt, anger, and betrayal in his wife eyes. Looking back, King wished he would have just been honest and upfront with his wife months ago. Mya laughed, "Imagine my surprise when I got home this morning to find this in the mailbox!", she said, while hitting King across the face with a stack of pictures. King looked down when a few of the photos fell from Mya's hand, and landed on the bed. His mouth opened in shock, "That devious bitch!", he thought. In the photos, King's head was thrown back in pleasure, which explains how he didn't see the tramp taking the pictures. She had planned this all along. How had he let that sneaky bitch manipulate him into hurting the only woman he truly loved. Mya was his soulmate, his gift from God. "Mya, I Love you baby", he gently said. Mya sat quietly as she looked down and stared into her husband eyes. How had they got to this point? Just one year ago, they were saying "I Do!", in front of their family and friends during a gorgeous wedding ceremony. The man she gave her virginity too, the man she vowed to love for better or for worse. King and Mya were supposed to be on a flight headed to Hawaii in just a few hours to celebrate their one-year anniversary. But that would never happen now. There would be no celebrations, this year, or any other year for that matter. "If you really loved me, you wouldn't have put your dick in that nasty bitch!", she screamed, just before pulling the trigger on the gun, filling the room with nothing but silence.

Chapter 1

"Uggggh, I'm sick of this nigga shit"! Mya screamed, throwing her phone against the bedroom room wall. The expensive I-phone hit the wall and shattered into a hundred tiny pieces. "Why does he keep doing me like this", she wondered out loud? Since the day she met her husband King, Mya had dedicated herself to be her husband ride or die. Things weren't always this bad between her and King. In the beginning he was a sweet, loving, respectful man, who kept her on a pedestal. But after putting up with King lies, secret phone calls, and long hours in the streets for the past couple of months, Mya was starting to feel maybe it was time for her to let go and move on with her life. She had watched her mother be a perfect wife to her father for twenty years. The same father who walked out of their life, for his twenty-something year old blond, big boob, ex-stripper, secretary. With only a high-school diploma, Mya watched as her mother, worked two jobs, struggling to make ends meet, while the man she dedicated over half of her life to for years, moved on without so much of a glance back. Mya vowed not to make the same mistakes her mother had made, but here she was, with King doing the exact same shit. At the age of twenty-five Mya considered herself to be a dime piece. With rich chocolate skin, light brown eyes, and hair that reached her voluptuous ass when she straightened it, she was often mistaken for a stripper or video vixen. Mya snickered, thinking back on the day her and King met. Mya and her best friend Star were walking to their car after enjoying a lady's day at the spa, when an all-black Benz, with tinted windows pulled up beside them. The two ladies sped up their pace, as the driver slowly rolled the front window down. "Excuse me ladies", Mya heard a voice call out through the window but kept walking. Mya had just landed her dream job as an entry-level financial advisor with one of Michigan's top marketing firms and dating right now was the furthest thing from her mind. For Star, it only took one glance at the luxury car to cause a slow in her stride. She was always on the prowl for a new "sponsor" and was not about to pass up the opportunity to meet "new-money". "One second girl this might be the meal ticket I've been waiting on", Star whispered to Mya as the shiny black on black vehicle pulled over to the side of the road. Mya shook her head and pulled out her cell phone to check her text messages while she waited to the side for her girl to do her thing. She never understood why Star would whether use men to finance her instead of using her bachelor's degree in administration to finance herself. Mya glanced up from her phone when she heard a deep baritone voice behind her say, "I'm Pretty sure I'm more interesting then what's in that phone!" Mya was unsure of what to say looking at the tall, chocolate, well-built man sexy man towing over her, licking his full sexy lips. Before she could gather her thoughts, Star approached the two, "Hi, I'm Star she said, extending her hand. "King!", he flatly told her, before turning his attention back to Mya. Star was shocked to say the least. She could tell by King's swag he was a certified boss. Star loved her girl, but she knew Mya would have no clue on what to do with a man like that being she was still an inexperienced virgin. Star waited for Mya to casually dismiss him being that she had shown an interest in him first but was surprised to see King had Mya blushing and giggling like a schoolgirl. By the time King walked away, he and Mya had exchanged numbers and set up a dinner date for the next night. "You are okay with us going out right?", Mya asked Star once King had jumped in his car and pulled off. Star didn't want to come across as a hater to her girl by admitting she did have a problem with her and King going out. It won't go far anyway, Star thought. There was no way a plain jane girl like Mya would be able to keep a man like King attention for too long. "Girl, my roster of niggas is full", Star shrugged. "I couldn't take on another one anyway!" Mya studied her friend face for a moment. After all the years the two had known each other, Mya couldn't help but to feel like there was a lot more to Star that she didn't know.

Mya and Star met during their freshman year of college and hit it off right away. Because they had a few of the same classes together they would often meet in study hall and prepare for tests. Star was a beautiful girl, with creamy skin the color of buttermilk, hazel green eyes, short curly honey blond hair, a small waist, thick hips, and an ass so round it didn't look like it belonged on her body. Between Mya's rich dark complexion and Star's creamy milk tone, the two became known on campus as "vanilla and chocolate". Because they had a few classes together the girls would often meet up at study hall and prepare for tests. By their last year of college, Mya and Star had moved into an off-campus apartment, where Mya stayed focused on her studies and barely dated while Star hardly attended class and dated just about every football player on campus. Star was always looking to "secure a bag", so she attached herself to nearly every athlete on campus just in case they made it to the pros. Mya graduated with honors, receiving a bachelor's degree in Business while Star received her bachelor's degree in Administration but only after orally pleasing two of her male professors for the passing grade she needed in order to graduate. Despite their differences the two friends grew close over the years and confided in each other about everything. Mya didn't agree with Star promiscuous behavior but didn't judge her for it. Mya figured something in Star past was the cause of her "Fuck Niggas, Get Money Attitude". There were times Star would become distant and stand- offish out the blue. Whenever Mya would try to get her to open-up about what was wrong, Star would become defensive. Mya loved Star and

only wanted the best for her friend. She prayed one day
Star would realize that.

Chapter 2

Mya stood in front of the full- length mirror in her bedroom as she admired her reflection. The white mini bodycon dress she wore hugged her thick body like a glove and accented her curves in all the right places. Mya decided to pin her hair up in a high bun on top of her head with a few loose tresses falling around her face. Her makeup was done to perfection and gave her skin a nice soft glow. "Well what do you think?", she asked Star who was sitting at the foot of her bed flipping through a magazine. Star barely looked up before throwing a flat, "Cute!", Mya's way. "Are you sure you are okay with me going out with King?", Mya sincerely asked. "I saw you batting those long eyelashes at him", she laughed, while blinking her eyelashes exaggeratedly, trying to lighten the moment. "Honestly, he is a little too dark for my liking! Bright is right!", Star said rubbing her light-colored knees, through the holes of the ripped jeans she had on. For a moment, Mya just stood there as Star smiled at her knowing she had just gotten under Mya's skin. Being ridiculed as a child for being dark skin, Mya was sensitive to jokes concerning her skin tone. She had shared this with Star one night back in college while the two were writing a paper on racism. Mya now regretted doing so because sometimes she felt Star was intentionally trying to hurt her with dark skin jokes. "Girl please!", Mya laughed, "Those knees black as me now with how much you stay on them!". Mya was pleased to see she had knocked the smirk off Star's face. She loved her best friend, but she wasn't going to let anybody talk crazy to her, friend or not. The room was filled with an awkward silence as Mya strapped the laces of her Giuseppe heels around her leg. Mya wasn't going to let Star nasty attitude ruin her night.

Just as Mya finished lacing the last string around her leg, the doorbell rang. "He's Here!", she excitedly squealed.

"Star go get the door for me while I freshen up my lip gloss!", Mya said. Star rolled her eyes and stomped out the room. She walked down the stairs, flung the door open and walked away, leaving King standing in the doorway unsure of what to do. King stepped inside and walked in the same direction he saw Star go in. He sat the roses down he purchased for Mya and took a seat on the couch across from Star. "I'm assuming she will be down in a minute?", he asked with a smirk. Star barely muttered "Yeah!", as she grabbed a magazine off the coffee table and started flipping through it. When Star heard King mumble "Bitter Bitch!", she looked up from the magazine. "Did you just call me a bitch?" King just stared at her. She was the typical pretty, gold-digging bitch, with a bad attitude jealous of anyone who was being shown more attention than her. He could spot women like her a mile away. "Damn he finer then I remember", Star thought while staring him down. Star stood up to go the kitchen making sure King had a good view of her plump ass in the tight jeans she wore. She was disappointed when she looked back thinking he would be staring at her ass only to find him flipping through the same magazine she had just put down. "You not my type bitch", he chuckled, never looking her way.

King was in awe as Mya descended the stairs. Mya was a goddess. Not only was she beautiful with a curvy body, she also carried herself classy and ladylike. Mya innocence combined with her sex appeal gave her a mysterious allure. King had been with his share of women in the past, but none had made him even think twice about settling down until now. King and his best friend/ business partner Don built an empire across the city of Detroit over the past ten years. They had territory from the east to west side and was the major supplier of over half the drugs that flooded the city. At the age of thirty King was now thinking about his future. He had made millions of dollars since being in the game and invested his money very wisely. With all the properties King now owned all over the city, he could comfortably retire whenever he desired. Although King desperately wanted children, after watching so many of his homeboys lose their freedom and life at the hands of ratchet, emotional, bitter ass women, he refused to have a baby with just anyone. King didn't want just a baby mother, he wanted a wife and family. But first, he had to find a woman worthy of that title. He was a certified street nigga and had flocks of women fighting for the "wife title" in his life but for all the wrong reasons. He would never serve as someone "meal-ticket", just for them to leave him high and dry if he ever got caught in a tight situation. King was in the streets and he accepted what came along with it. Death and long prison terms was always a possibility in the game. He needed a woman who would be by his side through thick and thin, not one who would be off in search of the next nigga with hefty pockets during hard times. Something told King Mya just may be what he has been looking for. King took Mya by the hand and escorted her out the door. Watching the sway of her ass in the tight dress that adorned her body had him hypnotized. King helped Mya into the car, brushing his hand against her soft skin as he closed the car door. As he walked to his side of the car, King looked back and caught a glimpse of Star standing in the door with scowl on her face. He made a mental note to warn Mya about her so called "best friend". He didn't know how Mya could miss the vibes of jealousy and hate that were bouncing off Star, but King could feel them from day one. He was baffled how the two women were even best friends, when they were obviously as opposite as night and day.

Mya and King made small talk while they headed to the restaurant. Mya was surprised with how at ease she felt around King and was glad there was no awkward silence between the two of them. When the old school hit "You're All I Need" by Mary J Blige and Method Man came on the radio, the two sang and rapped along like pros.

Like sweet morning dew

I took one look at you

And it was plain to see

You were my destiny

With you I'll spend my time

I'll dedicate my life, I'll sacrifice for you

Dedicate my life to you

You're all, I need

To get by

You're all, I need

King was impressed that Mya knew the entire song, word from word. He was glad to see she was classy but in touch with her hood side as well. King pulled into the restaurant and ran around to Mya's side of the car to open the car door for her. After handing his keys to valet, King placed his arm around Mya's waist and guided her through the restaurant towards the glass staircase that led up to the rooftop. Mya gasped when they stepped outside onto the patio area. All the tables had been removed from the area except one, which was sitting in the middle of the rooftop surrounded by candles and rose petals. As they took their seat at the table, a violinist came over stood on the side of them and began to play his violin softly. King snapped his fingers and two waiters rushed over and placed two crystal trays down in front of them. Mya's mouth watered at the sight of the huge lobster tails, scallops, and crab cakes that filled the tray. "How did you know seafood was my favorite?", she blushed, looking up at King. "A man always takes an interest in something he values". Mya was impressed by the efforts King had made for a beautiful first date. The two enjoyed the rest of their dinner chatting and listening to the violinist play, combined with the beautiful sounds of the river. King admired Mya's natural beauty as her hair blew softly in the wind. Mya did something to him no woman had ever done before which was gave him a sense of peace. After their first date, King and Mya became inseparable. King was a busy man, but he always made time for Mya. He sent flowers to her job, surprised her with weekend get-a-ways, and romantic picnics in the park. For the first time in his life King was in love.

Chapter 3

King was sprawled across Mya's bed watching the play-
offs, while Mya laid in his lap flipping through the latest
celebrity magazine. Mya loved checking out the latest
styles in the fashion world. As a teenager Mya would
design clothes for all the girls in her neighborhood. By her
senior year she had a full clientele. When Mya went away
to college, she put her love for fashion on hold to pursue
her degree in Business. Mya was proud of her degree in
Business but still had dreams of one day opening her own
business. "Isn't this cute?", Mya asked King, showing him
a picture of a run-way model that was rocking the latest
Givenchy Spring collection. "Not as cute as you"! Mya
blushed at King's words. King had a way of making her
feel like a queen. King leaned in and begin placing kisses
on Mya neck while massaging her thigh through the thin
pajama bottoms, she had on. When Mya felt his hand trying
to slide under her shorts, she stopped him. "Wait Baby!",
Mya breathed heavily. King pulled back, although he
desperately wanted Mya, he also respected her decision to
wait. Mya sat up and looked King in the eye. "I have
something I need to tell you!" King heart begin thumping
loudly in his chest. He prayed what she had to say wasn't
bad news. He loved Mya dearly, but he would not hesitate
to kill her in a heartbeat if she had deceived him in anyway.
Honesty was always a must with him. "I'm a virgin", Mya
whispered. King mouth dropped open in shock. It was
almost unheard of for a woman to reach Mya's age
untouched. King leaned in and softly kissed her. "I'll wait
for as long as you want baby!". He knew right then and
there, he was going to make Mya his wife, *if and only if*,
they received his mother blessings.

"How do I look baby?", Mya nervously asked while
standing in front of King. Her and King were having lunch
with his mother this afternoon and Mya wanted to make a

good first impression. Mya really loved King and hoped his mother could see she wasn't just another groupie, after his coins. After six months of dating Mya could see King was a rich and powerful man but she also saw a lot more to him than that. King was also loving, funny, compassionate, and sweet. At first, Mya was bothered when her and King went out together and women showed no respect for her or themselves for that matter, practically throwing themselves at his feet. Mya admired King for always making her feel secure in her position. "Baby you're beautiful!" "Stop Worrying I'm sure my mother is going to love you!" Mya turned to look at her ass in the mirror. "You don't think the skirt is too much?", she asked. Mya loved how the snug pencil skirt hugged her curves and she complimented the skirt with a soft pink off the shoulder blouse. King grabbed Mya waist from behind and buried his nose into the groves of her neck. He loved inhaling her sweet scent. Mya blushed, looking at their image in the mirror and silently thanked God for sending her the man of her dreams. She grabbed her clutch bag and the two were on their way.

King and Mya entered the outside patio dining area, hand in hand. His mother had already arrived and was sitting at the table sipping on a glass of mimosa. "Sorry we are running a few minutes late mama!", King said leaning down to give his mother a kiss. "Let me guess Ms. Mya here changed clothes about ten times looking for just the perfect outfit to meet me in!", she laughed. The three broke into laughter as Mya extended her hand to King's mother. "Nice to meet you Ms. Davis", she politely said. King's mother pulled her in for a hug, "Girl Ms. Davis is my mother!" "Call me Brenda or Mama Brenda!" Mya and King smiled at each other and took a seat. Mya was happy that King's mother was warm and friendly. She learned, like her mother King's mother raised him alone after his father walked out on them. King had also watched his mother struggle to provide for him and vowed to one day give her everything her heart desired. Before King purchased his own home, he brought his mother a four-bedroom, three-bathroom, home in Canton a quiet suburban neighborhood right outside the city of Detroit. His mother had put him first her entire life, now it was King's turn to show her his appreciation. Because his mother loved to read King had an indoor patio with a jacuzzi and fireplace installed in the back of her home. King's mother was the apple of his eye and any women in his life would have to accept that.

Chapter 4

King enjoyed his lunch in silence while he sat back and watched his mother and Mya interact. He couldn't help but to rejoice at how well the two women got along. From their chit-chat and giggles, one would have thought the two women had known each other for years. By the time the trio finished eating Mya and his mother had exchanged telephone numbers with the promise of getting together soon for a "girls-day". Ms. Brenda gave her son a subtle wink as they exited the restaurant. King knew that was his mother's way of giving him Mya's approval. King was very protective of his mother and rarely brought anyone around to meet her. He valued his mother opinion because he knew she always would have his best interest at heart. Outside of Mya, King's mother had only met one other woman he dated, and her name was Stacey.

Flashback

King truly thought Stacy was the love of his life, but his mother saw right through her from the start. King and Stacey knew each other from their neighborhood. Stacy was a pretty, quiet girl who always kept to herself. If you didn't see her walking to and from school, you probably would not know she existed. King was always drawn to a woman who didn't go out of their way to be seen or heard, it made them appear more ladylike in his eyes. After silently watching Stacy from a distance for years, he built up the courage to ask her to prom. Stacy was hesitant at first because she knew about King's bad boy image in the neighborhood, but eventually agreed to go out with him. King and Stacy went to prom together and stayed on the dance floor the entire night. After prom, King took Stacy to an expensive downtown restaurant where the two feasted on a five-course meal. King was a perfect gentleman making sure Stacy was home by curfew, walking her to the front door and giving her a peck on the cheek. The two stayed in touch when Stacy went off to college and whenever Stacy came home to visit, they would spend the entire time together. At Stacy's college graduation King asked her to officially be his girl. He was now heavy in the drug game and making serious money and the only thing missing in his life was his ride or die chick. Stacy moved into King's luxurious six-bedroom downtown condominium and King made sure she didn't want for anything. He purchased her a brand-new G-wagon truck and provided her with his black card to go shopping whenever her heart desired. King only asked for appreciation, loyalty and honesty in return. The day King took Stacy to meet his mother, his mother had refused to say more than hi over dinner. King's mother was normally a friendly woman unless it was something about you, she just didn't like. After dropping Stacy off, King decided to go pay his mother a visit.

"Ma!", King screamed, as he walked into her home. "Boy stop all that damn yelling! "I'm in the kitchen!". King found his mother sitting at her kitchen table eating a bowl of chocolate chip ice-cream. "Ma, I thought you were cutting back on sweets?", King asked while grabbing a spoon out the kitchen drawer. He pulled up a chair next to his mother and dug himself a scoop of ice cream from her bowl. King's mother already knew what her son was there for, the cold shoulder she had given his little "girlfriend" at dinner. Ms. Brenda could spot a snake a smile away and Stacey was a python. She could tell Stacy was a gold-digger and only after one thing, King's money. While Ms. Brenda was ready for her only child to settle down and start a family, she wanted it to be with someone who deserved him. She knew if King married Stacy, it would be the worst mistake of his life. "I don't like her!", Ms. Brenda flatly said. King ate another spoon of ice cream

before responding. "It's not what you are thinking ma!" "Don't you remember her from the neighborhood?", he asked. When his mother didn't reply, he continued. "She has a good head on her shoulders with a college degree!". Ms. Brenda pushed the bowl of ice cream away from her and looked directly in her son eyes. "Has she ever tried to put that college degree to work?" "Has she even once mentioned looking for a job?" "Education means nothing if she doesn't know what to do with it!" "How many times have she talked about you getting out the game?" "A woman that truly loves a man would push for him to have a plan for one day making it out the streets, with his life and freedom!". King sat and quietly listened while taking in everything his mother was saying. After really thinking about it, he couldn't recall one-time Stacy had ever said anything about looking for a job. And the only thing he remembered discussing about their future was her desire for a bigger house although they were already staying in a huge six-bedroom home, with just the two of them. "I hear you ma, and I'll keep everything you said in mind!" "All I'm asking is for you to give her a fair chance!". Kings mother gave her son a tight, firm hug, "I only give chances to the people who deserve it!"

Chapter 5

For the next few months King spent more time with Stacy in hopes of proving his mother feelings wrong, however the more he opened his eyes and looked, the more things he saw that he didn't like. Over breakfast one morning King casually brought up Stacy looking for a job. "Well Ms. College Degree you graduated almost a year ago maybe it's time you put all that hard work into action". King studied Stacy closely while waiting on her response. Stacy popped a small piece of pop tart in her mouth before responding. "Work for what?", she snootily asked. "I have a KING that provides all my needs!" For the first time King saw something in Stacy that he didn't like, ungratefulness. He didn't know how he missed it before when the signs were so obvious. "What if something happens to me?" "How will you survive if you have never worked before?", King curiously asked. When Stacy casually replied, "Off whatever stash you leave me", King knew his mother was right. Stacy didn't love him, she loved what he did for her. Unbeknownst to King, while away at college Stacy heard how King was rapidly coming up in the streets from her old neighborhood friends. Before hearing this Stacy had no desire of being anything more than friends with King. She was already dating the star basketball player on campus and was just waiting for him to be drafted into the pros and become his trophy wife. Stacy never allowed King to visit her while she was away at school because she was determined to keep the two men from finding out about each other. She never believed putting all her eggs in one basket was a smart thing to do and had no problem stringing both men along until she knew which situation would benefit her the best. When Stacy college sweetheart was injured during a game one night and told he may never play basketball again she made her decision. Without even a goodbye to him, Stacy graduated and moved right in with King.

Stacy had no plans of working ever! She stood from the table and sashayed over to King. As she straddled his lap and massaged the growing bulge in his jeans. "If I get a job, I wouldn't have time to do this", she whispered in his ear dropping to her knees in front of him. As she took him into her warm mouth King reached down and begin to guide her head. This is exactly how Stacy had secured her position in the first place, her head game was on point. King pushed the thought of how many dicks she must have sucked to get so good at it to the back of his head. Stacy begin to suck faster when she felt his body stiffen up letting her tongue slide between the slit on his head. King toes curled as his nut begin to build up. The way Stacy slithered her tongue around had him ready to go insane. Stacy caught every drop when King finally exploded in her mouth. "That should keep him quiet for a while", she thought as she stood to her feet and headed to the bathroom to brush her teeth. King wasn't a fool, he knew exactly what Stacy was doing. She had just proved his mother right but her superb dick sucking skills would only earn her the title as his main hoe not his wife. That night King walked into their bedroom and found Stacy laying in the middle of their bed naked playing on her phone. The sight of her naked body almost made him forget the words he had been rehearsing in his head all day. "Hey daddy", Stacy sung, flipping onto her stomach. The sight of her round ass jiggling in the air made him stiff instantly. Stay focused, he mentally told himself. "Stacy this!", he said pointing between the two of them, "Is not working". "What!", Stacy yelled jumping off the bed. "What do you mean this isn't working?" "Don't I fuck and suck you anytime you ask?" King shrugged his shoulders, "I can get that anywhere; do you know who I am?" "What else do

you have to offer?" When Stacy didn't respond, King knew he was making the right decision. "I already found you a nice three-bedroom apartment in a gated community".
"You can keep the G-wagon and I'll still make sure you have a small spending allowance for the next year", King said. "So, I've been degraded to your hoe", she smirked while putting it all together. "A hoe with great benefits!", King retorted. After thinking it over for a moment Stacy laid back on the bed and spread her legs wide open. King looked on in lust as she starting to play with herself. The deal was sealed when she asked, "When do I start?" Stepping closer to the bed King begin stripping out his clothes. "This is only for a year!" "You should have found a job by then!". A year was fine with Stacy, by then she would have found a new sponsor not a job.

Chapter 6

Although Stacy and King no longer communicated with each other King appreciated the valuable lesson that he learned from her. He now knew what qualities to look for in a woman! Mya possessed everything King desired in a wife. Not only was she beautiful, intelligent and smart, she also had goals for her future. Her being a virgin was just the cherry on top. King took pride in the fact he would be Mya's first and that alone made Mya worthy to be put on a pedestal. King smiled as he looked down at the 8-karat, princess cut, diamond ring he had custom made for Mya. Tonight, King was throwing Mya a surprise birthday party where he would ask her to become his wife. With the help of his mother King had turned his backyard into an elegant, cozy atmosphere. Small tables were spread throughout the backyard each one covered with white silk tablecloths and floating candles. Soft spot lights were lined along the make shift dancefloor that was set-up in the middle of the backyard. A live band set on one side of the dance floor with a live DJ on the other. Three huge buffet tables filled with Italian, Mexican, American and Cuban Food, took up the entire patio area. King checked his watch realizing he only had a couple of hours before it was time to pick up Mya. He walked over to where his mother and Mya's mother were finishing up the last of the decorations. Mya's mother was thrilled the day King stopped by her house to ask for her daughter hand in marriage. She could tell King was a good man and that he genuinely loved her daughter. After being sworn to secrecy, she agreed to help King and his mother pull off the surprise proposal. Ms. Brenda and Mya's mother bonded right away. Both women were ecstatic their children had found true love. King gave both women a kiss on the cheek, "Less talk, more work!", he joked while walking away. Ms. Brenda turned and playfully swatted her son on the butt. "You are never too old for a good old-fashioned ass whooping!", Ms. Brenda laughed. She caught how Star was staring at her son as he walked in the house. "I don't trust that bitch!", she mumbled. Mya's mother didn't even have to ask who Ms. Brenda was referring too. With her back still turned she said, "You must be talking about the one and only Star". Mya's mother visited her daughter often while she was away in college and it was something that just didn't sit well with her about Mya's roommate/best friend Star. Both mothers agreed they would have to keep an eye on Star because she could definitely become a problem in the future.

King sent his mother a quick text to inform her they were pulling down the street and to have the band cut the music. He knew the party was in full swing from looking at his home cameras through an app on his phone an hour ago. A luxury shuttle bus had picked up each guest from their home to ensure no cars were in the driveway and arouse Mya's suspicion. "I thought we had reservations at the restaurant for 7 p.m. babe?", Mya asked, as they pulled into the circular driveway of King's home. "We do I just have to run in the house and change my shirt right quick!", King nonchalantly said while getting out the car. King took Mya's hand as they made their way into the house. While heading up the stairs King stopped midway and yelled down to Mya, "Baby can you cut the lights on in the backyard while I grab my shirt?" "I don't want it to be dark around the house when we get in tonight!" "The switch is right on the outside of the patio door!" King prayed that Mya wouldn't see any silhouettes moving around as she approached the patio door. Just as Mya slid the patio door back the spotlights came on and everybody yelled out "Surprise!". Mya was so shocked that she turned to run back inside the house crashing right into King. "Where are you going?", he laughed. King grabbed Mya by the waist and led her back outside. Tears cascaded down her face as she looked around and saw her mother, Ms. Brenda, Don, Star, a few of her college friends and some of her co-workers scattered around the backyard. Mya walked around giving everyone a hug while 50 cent hit "It's Your Birthday", blared from the DJ's speakers. When she finally made her way back over to King she jumped in his arms and planted kisses all over his face. "I can't believe you did all this for me!", she beamed. King lightly kissed her on the forehead and said the "The best is yet to come!". He guided Mya to the middle of the dance floor and raised his hand. In an instant the DJ music stopped, and the live band began to softly play in the background. The DJ walked up to King and handed him a microphone while Mya stood there in suspense. First, I want to thank everyone for coming out to celebrate my baby Mya's birthday. King waited while everyone gave Mya a round of applause. Both Mya and King's mother walked onto the dance floor and stood on each side of the couple. Mya almost fainted when King dropped to his knees in front of her and pulled out a small black velvet box. "Mya, Will You Marry Me?" The entire backyard gasped as King opened the small box revealing the biggest diamond Mya had ever saw in her life. The diamond sparkled beautifully under the spotlights. Mya was so overtaken by emotions she couldn't form any words, all she could do was nod her head yes. King slid the huge ring on Mya's finger then stood up and grabbed Mya and both their mothers in for a hug. This was one of the happiest days of his life. Mya looked around for Star and wondered why her friend wasn't on the dance floor celebrating with her. When she finally spotted Star at one of the buffet tables making a plate, she made her way over to her.

Star was so busy angrily throwing food onto her plate that she didn't hear Mya approach her from behind. "Don't pile too much food on that plate!" "I need my maid of honor to keep her sexy figure!", Mya joked grabbing a shrimp off Star's plate. Star mustered up as much of a fake smile as she could. "Congratulations Bestie!" "You must have finally put it on him to seal the deal!" Mya let out an exaggerated sigh, "He fell in love with what was in my heart Star not what's between my legs!" "The key to everything is not always sex!", Mya scolded. "Excuse me, Ms. Goody, Goody!", Star said while turning to storm off, but Mya grabbed her by the arm and stopped her. "I'm not trying to judge you Star!" "I love you!" "And I only want what's best for you". "You deserve a good man, who will love you for you!" "You have an education dammit use it!" "Instead of using what's between your legs!" Mya's words stung Star to the core because she knew they were true. Is that what her so called best friend thought of her? A high-class prostitute? "How dare Mya sit up on her high horse and look down at people?", Mya fumed. Not everyone had a loving mother who put their child's needs before theirs. Mya didn't know shit about the awful things Star had to endure in life just to survive. Star saw the way Mya's mother turned her nose up at her whenever she came to visit Mya on campus. Mya and her mother were best friends and did everything together. Star envied their relationship because she lacked a relationship with her own mother. Star had not seen her mother since the day she packed her bags and headed off to college. If Mya only knew all the degrading things Star had done just to afford her college tuition, she probably wouldn't keep bringing up Star's "college degree". If it had not been for her married sixty-year-old boyfriend Richard, Star would not have been able to attend college in the first place.

Chapter 7

Flashback

Star met Richard the summer before her Freshman year in college. He was a lawyer at a prestigious downtown law firm, where she applied for a receptionist position. Financial aid was covering part of her tuition, but Star desperately needed this job to cover the difference of her tuition and her dorm cost. Star sat across from Richard admiring his salt and pepper beard as he glanced over her resume. Star seductively crossed her legs causing the dress she wore to creep up her thighs, revealing she wore no panties underneath. After glancing over her resume and seeing Star had no experience Richard cut right to the chase. He kept his focus on Star's perky breast while asking "You have no experience, why should we hire you?" Star stood up and smirked while walking over to the door and locking it. She slid her dress over her head and stood directly in front of Richard. "I have a lot of things I'm experienced at!", she said, licking her lips. Star thought the old man was about to have a heart attack as beads of sweat rolled down his face. He loosened his tie as Star pushed some papers off his desk and perched herself on top of it. She spun around and spread her legs making sure her neatly shaved peach was within inches of Richard's face. Star gently sucked on her index finger and began massaging her clit. At the age of sixty Richard had not seen a young pretty pussy in years and his tongue hung out of his mouth at the beautiful sight. Before he knew it, Richard found himself face first between Star's thick legs. Richard was a playboy back in his day and by the way Star was thrashing around on his desk, he had not lost his touch. After Star came twice Richard bent her over his desk and plunged into her so hard the desk almost fell over. Star tightness and warmth was sending him over the edge with each stroke. He panted and grunted as he gripped Star waist and delivered powerful strokes. When Star felt herself about to cum again, she buried her head in some papers, to keep from screaming out. "Damn this old man good!", she thought! Two orgasms later and Richard was in love. By the time Star left Richard's office, she had secured her job as his mistress instead of his receptionist. He purchased Star a new car, brought her expensive jewelry and faithfully paid her college tuition every semester. Richard felt like the man whenever he brought Star around his co-workers and friend and constantly boasted about how good his pretty little young thing was in bed. When Richard's boss offered him a promotion in exchange for one night with Star, he happily agreed. Star was reluctant at first but when Richard threatened to stop her tuition payments unless she went along with it, she agreed. One night turned to many, as Richard was offered perk after perk by different senior partners in exchange for a night with Star. Richard rapidly climbed the ladder of his law firm while Star was passed from one senior partner to another. By the time Star graduated college, Richard had made it to senior partner, with every upper lawyer having a turn between Star's legs.

As Star sat across from Richard in the exquisite five start restaurant her mind was a thousand miles away. She couldn't believe Mya and King would be marrying this weekend. Just thinking about how King went all out with his big fancy proposal made Star sick to the stomach. Last night Mya had stopped by Star's house unannounced with a bottle of wine and Chinese takeout. Mya noticed how distant her, and Star were becoming and felt like a little girl's time was needed. For two hours Star sat and listened to Mya endlessly ramble about wedding colors, menus, dresses, venues, and of course her and King's "over the top honeymoon" they had planned. Star spun the chicken fried rice around in her bowl as she listened to Mya gush over how King promised her a wedding of the lifetime with no spared expense. "Of course, having my best friend by my side for the happiest day of my life means the world to me!" Mya beamed while reaching for her purse. "Before I forget I have something for you", she said pulling a small Tiffany box from her purse and handing it to Star. They both remained quiet as Star unwrapped the box and opened it. Inside was a diamond tennis bracelet with the word "Best" inscribed on the inside. Mya rolled the sleeve of her shirt back revealing an identical diamond tennis bracelet but on the inside of hers was the word "Friend". "Now we will have something that links us together forever!", Mya squealed. "Married or not, you will always be my best friend!" Mya said, standing and wrapping her arms around Star's neck, "I Love You, Star Bright!" Star had to admit; the bracelet was stunning. Mya must have paid a pretty penny for it but probably at King's expense! Star snapped the bracelet around her wrist, "I love you too! She barley mumbled. Star was glad when Mya cell phone began ringing so she wouldn't catch the lack of enthusiasm in Star's voice.

Mya's face lit up like a Christmas tree when she answered the phone. "Hey baby!", she cooed, while plopping down on Star's soft leather sofa. Star watched in envy as Mya giggled on the phone with King while holding up her ring finger at different angles admiring the huge engagement ring. The deep V-neck sundress Mya wore made her full breast sit-up nice and perky and the cream color of the material made her chocolate skin glow. Why does she get to have it all? Star fumed while staring at her friend. Every time Mya called Star, she was bragging about a new piece of jewelry King had brought her or an exotic trip the two were going on. The fact that Mya had yet to sleep with King only infuriated Star more. Here she was sucking dick, licking ass, and fulfilling all type of sick sex fetishes just to get a few raggedy ass bills paid here and there while Mya was being given all the things Star dreamed of. King should have been hers. She should have been the one getting the royal treatment. Had Mya not thrown herself at King that day Star had no doubt in her mind he would have chosen her. Ever since the two of them had known each other Mya always had to be the center of attention. Mya was the student with straight A's, the campus sweetheart, the one with a great mom who paid her college tuition and came to visit her, the virgin because she wanted to wait on marriage. In just about everybody eyes Mya was perfect and could do no wrong.

Chapter 8

Mya could not have asked for more perfect weather on her wedding day. Their wedding ceremony would take place at sunset on a beautiful private lakefront resort. The lush patio garden was surrounded by 100-foot beautiful palm trees that provided an intimate setting. A cascading waterfall sat in the middle of fifty white linen chairs that were draped with silver sashays. A huge arch made from white silk flowers wrapped around the outdoor gazebo where Mya and King would take their vows. The guest was asked to wear all white, to enhance the all-white décor. Mya's mother could not stop crying as she helped her only child get dressed for one of the most important days of her life. "My little girl is all grown-up!" "You look beautiful baby!", Mya's mother said as she admired how the breathtaking white silk chiffon mermaid style gown adorned her daughters' body. The five-foot-long train, handstitched in pearl and diamond embroidery was spread out beautifully across the dressing room. As Mya placed the crystal tiara on the center of her head, she silently thanked God for this day. Mya grabbed her phone off the vanity table and checked to see if she had any missed calls. "What's wrong baby?', her mother asked noticing the worried look on her daughter's face. "I haven't heard from Star all day!" "I hope everything is okay!" Ms. Brenda and Mya's mother glanced at each other. They wouldn't be surprised if the little heifer didn't bother to show up at all. It was obvious to everyone that Star was not the friend Mya thought she was. Star had shown up to the wedding rehearsal late and intoxicated last night. During the rehearsal Star made sure to brush her body up against King every chance she got. Star was the most dangerous kind of person. The one who pretended to be your friend but really was you biggest secret enemy. "I'm sure she will be here shortly", Ms. Brenda reassured Mya while patting her on the back. Mya was thankful to now have two mothers who loved her endlessly. The trio said a quick prayer before heading over to where the ceremony would take place.

Just as the organist begin to play, Star came casually strutting up looking gorgeous in her platinum silver gown. The plunging v neck was trimmed in the same pearls and diamonds that adorned Mya gown. The A-line dress complimented Star hourglass shape, fitting her curves like a glove. Star's make up was flawless, making her creamy butter scotch skin glow. "Oh my God Star you look amazing!", Mya squealed. "I was so scared you wasn't going to make it". Ms. Brenda and Mya's mother rolled their eyes waiting to hear what sorry excuse would come from Star's mouth for nearly not making her best friend's wedding. The truth was, Star had contemplated all morning if she would attend the wedding. After deciding there was no justified reason, she could possibly come up with for missing such an important occasion, she prepared herself at the last minute. "It's been an emotional day for me!", Star finally said, "It took me a little longer than expected to get myself together!" Star made sure to make her voice crack up a little, so her words sounded more believable. "Mya kissed Star on the cheek and held out her wrist, dangling the Best Friend Tennis bracelet. "Besties Forever!", she sang. Star placed her wrist next to Mya's. "Best friends forever", she weakly said. Star could feel both Mya's and King's mother burning a hole right through her. If looks could kill, Star would be dead right where she stood.

Star made sure to put an extra sway in her hips as she walked down the aisle. As she took her place under the gazebo, she discreetly blew a kiss in King's direction. King turned his head in disgust as he anxiously waited for the love of his life to appear. A thin white curtain was placed in front of where Mya would make her entrance. King gasped when the curtain lowered and Mya appeared, no words could explain how beautiful his soon to be wife looked. As Mya marched down the aisle to "Spend My Life with You", by Eric Benett there wasn't a dry eye in sight. After professing their love to each other and declaring to stick by each other side for better or worse King and Mya were pronounced as husband and wife.

After the ceremony, guests were ushered onto the 20,000 square foot yacht where the reception would be held. The yacht was equipped with ten guest suites, a spa room, and an indoor jacuzzi on the main level. The top level held two bars, a dance floor with flashing lights, and a ballroom. The yacht owner Max, who was also King's connect only allowed certain people access to the master suite located on the lower level. Unless previously told most guest, who boarded the yacht were not aware the master suite existed. King led Mya to the yachts captain's area. The large cozy space with three large plush reclining chairs, surround sounds, flat screen television and small mini-bar resembled more of a bachelor's pad instead of a captain' area on a boat. After speaking with the captain for a few moments King pushed a button on the side of one of the reclining chairs, revealing a marble staircase. Mya was unsure of what to expect as they made their way down the staircase. She was completely taken back when they reached the bottom of the stairs. Mya had no ideal this room even existed. King made sure Max did not mention the master suite located on the yacht the day him and Mya toured it. The drop-down ceiling was made of glass where Mya and King could see out, but people could not see in. An electric fireplace was built into the room and sat over a heart shaped jacuzzi. Mya was so busy admiring everything in the suite, it took her a minute to realize she was standing on a glass floor that allowed her to see directly into the ocean below. She squealed in delight as several colorful fish swam around under her feet. King quietly looked on thrilled he had given his wife the special day she dreamed of. "Let's get this reception over with baby!", Mya sexily said while trailing kisses along King's neck. "I'm ready to bless you with what you have been patiently waiting on!"

The reception was in full party mode by the time Mya and King entered the ballroom. The catering staff were dressed in cocktail gowns and tuxedos and were serving guests from crystal silver platters. Everyone marveled over the huge six tier wedding cake, sprinkled with edible glittery gems, and topped with K&M Swarovski letters. For the reception Mya changed into a simple and elegant knee length Ivory dress that was trimmed in soft feathers along the hemline. Mya and King mingled with their guest before taking a seat at the head table. Mya was happy to see Star had brought along a date for the evening. Although the gentleman seemed to be a tad on the older side, if Star was happy Mya was happy. After enjoying a five-course meal, the newlyweds shared a kiss under the moonlight during their first dance. Mya leaned in and whispered in her husband's ear. "Thank You for making this day magical, my King!" King was happy the day had turned out perfect. "Anything for my Queen!", he whispered in Mya's ear. As the song ended Don stood up and tapped his glass to get everyone attention. "I would just like to take a moment and officially welcome my sis to the family!" "You're making King an old softie!", he laughed before continuing. "Speaking as King's best friend, and on behalf of Ms. Brenda, we know he is good hands!" Ms. Brenda raised her glass in approval. "A toast to the newlyweds!" Don shouted. "To the newlyweds!", the guest happily yelled out. "I guess it's my turn Star slurred as she stood and grabbed the microphone out of Don's hand. Seeing that Star was tipsy, King subtly signaled for the DJ to cut the music back on. He was unsure of what Star would do or say, and he had worked too hard on making sure this day was perfect to let Star ruin it. King and Mya could barely keep their hands off each other during the reception. King secretly groped his wife under the table every chance he got anxious to get back to their suite. After cutting their wedding cake and making a champagne toast at midnight the two called it a night with their family and friends. They were ready to enjoy the rest of their night as husband and wife *alone*.

Chapter 9

Mya took a quick shower and slipped into the peach nightie she purchased for her honeymoon. She admired how the nightgown pushed up her large breast and accented her curvy hips and round ass. One look at Mya when she stepped out of the bathroom had King instantly rising through his Gucci boxers. As hard as it was King had stayed faithful to Mya the entire time, he waited for their wedding day. King had been in the streets long enough to know, the same loyal pussy, was better than swimming in and out of different pussy every night. King had his fair share of women in the past and knew he wasn't missing out on anything. He stared at his wife beauty knowing she had been worth every minute of the wait. Mya walked over to her husband and straddled his lap. The vanilla scent of her skin was intoxicating. The champagne Mya consumed all night calmed her nerves and relaxed her. She leaned in and licked King's bottom lips before sticking her tongue fully in his mouth. Their tongues intertwined into a beautiful rhythm neither one of them wanted to stop. The heat coming from between Mya's legs made King reach down and begin to massage her warmness through the thin lace panties she had on. When King slid a finger inside her Mya let out a slight moan. King stopped to make sure Mya was okay" I'm not hurting you am I baby?", he breathed heavily. When Mya shook her head no, King slid his finger back in her and begin stroking her clit in light circular motions. She lightly bit down on his shoulder as her body began trembling from her first orgasm. When King felt Mya's, body start to come down from the effects of the orgasm he stood up with her legs still wrapped around his waist and gently laid her back on the bed. He slipped Mya's nightie over her head and admired his wife fully nude body. Her rich chocolate skin was flawless, and he wanted to taste every inch of it.

King softly kissed Mya's lips before traveling down her neck. He caressed her full breast giving them each a light squeeze. He plopped one of her huge chocolate nipples in his mouth, gently sucking on it like a newborn baby. When Mya begin squirming around in delight, he moved further down her body. His tongue danced in and out her navel before lowering his head between her legs. He inhaled her sweet womanly scent before placing kissing on her inner thighs. King lightly nibbled on Mya's swollen clit before diving in head first. Mya cried out in ecstasy as King tongue twirled and licked around, as if he was searching for buried treasures. King firmly gripped Mya's hips, when he felt her legs begin to shake. "Cum baby!", he mumbled, never breaking his rhythm. That was all it took for Mya juices to flow everywhere. King happily licked up all his wife juices before crawling on top of her. "I love you", he whispered while gently easing himself into Mya's virgin hole inch by inch. When he felt Mya's body tense up, he stopped and softly kissed her. "Just relax Baby!" "I promise I won't Hurt You!" King kept a slow pace until he felt himself all the way in. Once she adjusted to King's size Mya began to rock her hips back and forth under King. The pain she was feeling at first, quickly turned to pleasure as she began to moan out her husband's name in pure pleasure. Mya was so wet and tight King had to pull out to keep from cumin prematurely. He waited a few seconds, before sliding back in," Damn Baby!", he moaned. He gently placed Mya's legs on his shoulders and dug deeper in her wetness. Mya's eyes rolled to the back of her head when King started hitting her G-spot. "Baby! Baby! I'm about to cum!", she screamed out. King pushed deeper into Mya and released all his seeds in her as far as they would go. He planned to have his wife pregnant by the end of their honeymoon. When both of their breathing slowed down, King laid down next to his wife and pulled her into a spoon position. He rubbed her hair until they both fell into a peaceful sleep.

Star was beyond drunk by the time her and Richard retired to their suite for the night. She should have been rejoicing that her best friend had such an amazing wedding day instead it angered her. The extravagant wedding only reminded Star how pathetic her life really was. For her entire life, Star had firmly believed in "using what she had, to get what she wanted". Star loved living the lavish life without having to work hard for it. She didn't mind letting different men run in and out of her, long as she enjoyed the perks that came along with it. The new cars, high-rise condominium and expensive jewelry made it all worthwhile, until now. Richard threats every time she refused to do something, or "someone" was a constant reminder that her whole lifestyle could be taken away from her in the blink of an eye. Watching King and Mya, Star was starting to desire more. She wanted a man who loved and adored her, how King loved and adored Mya. As much as Star tried, she could not get King's attention. The more King rejected her, the more determined Star became. She knew if she could put her tight warm gushy on him just one time, he would be all hers. Mya would just have to get with the program, the same way Richard's wife had too. Star laughed remembering the first time Richard's wife found out about her. *Star and Richard were in the middle of passionate sex in the same bed him and his wife shared for years. Richard's wife was supposed to be out to dinner with her friends until later that evening but returned home early not feeling well. Star's plump ass was damn near smothering Richard as she sat on his face enjoying how he sucked and licked on her clit. Just as Star was about to cum, Richard's wife came storming into the room. Richard tried to push Star off him but her thick thighs were locked around his head. Star didn't give a fuck if Santa Claus walked in the room, her orgasm was too close to stop. Richards's wife stood in the doorway crying as Star grinded her hips on top of Richard's face, until her body was rocking from a powerful orgasm. She didn't release Richard's head until every drop was released from her body. Star rolled over on the bed to catch her breath while Richard sat up wiping Star juices from his lips. "I didn't want you to find out this way, but I'm glad this is finally out in the open", he said. "This is my mistress Star!" Richard said, pointing over at Star who was still laying naked in the bed doing nothing to cover herself. "You either accept our relationship, or you can leave, but Star is here to stay!" his voice boomed in an authoritative manner. Richards's wife backed out of the room, informing them she would be waiting downstairs until they finished. For the rest of the night Richard fucked Star in every position possible, while his wife sat downstairs on the couch and painfully listened. Star made sure her moans were loud enough to put on a show.*

Chapter 10

The next morning Mya felt like she was floating on air as her and King left their suite to meet everyone for breakfast on the upper level of the yacht. "Somebody's glowing!", Ms. Brenda sang as she sat at the table with Mya's mother slicing a cream cheese bagel in half. Mya blushed "Stop it Mommy Brenda!" Mya skin glowed under the white halter sundress she was wearing. The soft breeze blew threw her hair giving her an angelic look. "Baby sit down, I'll make your plate", she told King. King mouth opened in shock; besides his mother no woman had ever offered to fix his plate before. "Close your mouth before something flies in it boy!", Ms. Brenda laughed. Mya piled King's plate with scrambled eggs, French toast, bacon and eggs. She wanted to make sure he had energy for part two tonight. Once Mya had King situated, she fixed herself a light plate of bacon and eggs and grabbed a seat at the table with everybody. While they devoured their food, they all laughed and talked about the highlights of the wedding. Mya looked around and noticed Star and Richard was nowhere in sight. The more Mya thought about it, outside of dinner last night she had barely saw Star since they had boarded the yacht. She started to ask if anyone had seen her but decided against it. Mya was growing tired of constantly asking about Star whereabouts. She was married now, and it was time she focused on her husband and her career. Star was grown and capable of making good decisions, whether she chose to or not was now completely up to her. After breakfast King and Mya enjoyed a couples' massage, while sipping on mimosas. King sighed, enjoying the firmness of the elderly Asian woman hands. It had been a while since he could fully relax. When he opened his eyes and glanced over at his wife, she was lovingly staring at him. "What's wrong Bae?" he asked. Mya slightly lifted her head up. "Just hoping this all not a dream I'm going to wake up from!"

The last two days, Mya felt like she was living in a fairy tale and had to pinch herself a couple of times to make sure she wasn't dreaming. King smiled at his wife, "You are not dreaming baby!" "A King's wife should always be treated like a Queen!" "All I ask is you always be honest and loyal!" To Mya that would be simple, she couldn't think of anything in the world that would make her betray a man who was so good to her.

While everyone else was enjoying breakfast, Star was in Don's suite shrieking in delight. After waking up with a slight hangover, Star slipped out of her suite in search of some aspirin and tonic water. Figuring the kitchen would be her best option to find what she needed, Star headed towards the stairs that led to the upper deck. "You really shouldn't be prancing around in such skimpy clothing!", she heard a voice say from behind her. Star was only wearing her lace bra and boy shorts figuring no one would be up this early after such a long night of partying. Star turned and came face to face with Don. She smirked, "Maybe you have what I'm looking for?" Star said stepping closer into his space. Don hesitated before responding, "Maybe!", he smirked while rubbing the growing bulge in his jogging pants. Don had a thing for red bones, especially thick ones. The more he took in Star's body in the lace bra and panty set, the more aroused he became. Star licked her lips "I'm dry do you have anything to hydrate me?", she teased. When Don turned on his heels and headed back to his suite, Star followed. Star had been so focused on King that she overlooked the next best thing, his partner. For the first time Star noticed how attractive Don was with his deep 360 waves and small dimples that played peek-a-boo through his smooth caramel colored skin when he smiled. Maybe attending this little wedding wasn't such a bad thing after all. Don grabbed two small orange juices out the mini fridge and poured them into a glass.

"Where is your daddy?", he joked, referring to the older man he overheard King and Mya's mom talking about, that Star had brought along as date. Don figured he must be Star's "sugar daddy", and she had only brought him along to fund her trip since he stayed tucked in their suite most of the time. "Exactly where he needs to be!", she sexily said while unhooking her bra. Don walked over to one of his suitcases, grabbed a wad of money out and threw it on the bed. He figured there was no need to beat around the bush.

Don knew Star type all too well. She was the type of woman after one thing, money. That was fine with him, Don had more money than he knew what to do with. He was happy his best friend had found the love of his life. King was a good man who deserved a good woman; however Don had no intentions of ever settling down with just one woman when he had a collection of beautiful women from state to state. He would decide if Star would be added to his collection, after sampling her goods. "Take them panties off and get on your knees!" he ordered. Star excitedly did as she was told, rushing to slip her panties down over her ankles and hoisting her ass in the air. Don gave Star ass two firm slaps before dipping inside her. "Damn"! he yelled out as he slid in and out of her. Don had slept with a lot of women, but none felt like this. Star bounced her ass and made it jiggle with every stroke Don made. Grabbing Star by the back of her neck, he sped up his pace when he felt himself about to cum. Don let out a loud grunt, before pulling out and releasing his seeds on Star back. He was adding Star to his collection, and maybe giving her the top spot.

Chapter 11

Star slipped back into her suite, hoping Richard would still be asleep. She was happy when she heard his light snores as she entered the room. Star jumped in the shower, hurrying to wash Don scent off her. Her pussy was still throbbing from the beating Don had just put on her. She couldn't wait to get back home and hit Somerset mall, ready to spend the money Don had just given her. Star hummed to herself as she lathered her body with her favorite cocoa scented bodywash. When she stepped out the bathroom, she jumped at the sight of Richard sitting up on the side of the bed. "Someone is in a good mood this morning!", he said, walking past Star to get into the bathroom for his morning rituals. Star was hoping she would be dressed and gone before he finished in the bathroom. She quickly put lotion on her body and slipped on her Dolce and Gabbana baby doll dress with the matching gold thong sandals. She accessorized the outfit with big Gold Hoop earrings and a light coat of gold lipstick. Once she gave herself a quick look over, she grabbed her clutch bag and headed towards the door. Just as her hand touched the door knob Richard stepped out of the bathroom naked. "Where do you think you going?"

"You were so drunk last night, you didn't take care of daddy!", he said while stroking himself. "I didn't pay for this expensive trip to not enjoy myself as well". Star rolled her eyes, trying to hide her irritation. "Baby I'm already dressed" she whined, "Can't it wait until we get back later?" "We still have one more night to enjoy ourselves!" Star walked over to Richard and replaced his hand with hers and started stroking him. She was praying he would not press the issue. Don was twice the size of Richard and there was no way Richard would not be able to tell she had just been bust wide open by Don if they had sex right now.

Richard pushed Star hand away, "This trip was seven

thousand dollars, which means I'll get my nut now and later!", he roared. Star tried to think fast. "And what if I refuse?", she boldly said. Richard chuckled, taking a seat on the bed, "Then I guess I would just refuse to pay your bill this month". This was just the shit Star hated! How Richard always threatened her the second she didn't do what he wanted. Star wanted to yell, "Fuck You!", now that she was pretty sure Don was on board but that was new, and she wasn't ready to depend on Don for security just yet. Star walked over to the bed and dropped to her knees between Richard legs. His dick was nice and hard and pointing straight at her. She moistened her mouth, then sucked him in like a vacuum. At the age of sixty, Richard was only capable of cuming once every few hours. If she could use her superb skills to drain him, she would have a few hours to do her Kegel exercises and snap her walls back into place. Star moaned and gagged just how Richard liked. The nastier she was the faster he would cum. When she heard him start to babble incoherently Star went all the way down making his dick touch her tonsils. When his cum shot to the back of her throat, she kept sucking until she caught every drop. Richard fell back on the bed completely out of breath. Star went into the bathroom, gurgled and touched up her lipstick. "Meet me upstairs for brunch", Star called out to Richard who was still sprawled out across the bed unable to move. She knew he would be sleep for hours.

Chapter 12

Flashback

From a young age, Star had to use her body in order to survive. She grew up in one of the grimmest projects in Detroit, The Herman Gardens. The only time she saw her crackhead mother was when she was turning tricks in their roach infested apartment for a few dollars. Star would be home alone for days at a time with only stale crackers and dirty faucet water to survive on. A couple of times a month she would catch the bus to Walmart and steal deodorant, soap and pads. The only clothes Star owned were hand me downs from her former best friend, Keisha. Keisha was jumping rope on the playground one day when she noticed a group of kids surrounding a girl teasing her. Keisha noticed the girl being teased was her classmate who normally sat in the back of the class, never talked to anyone and wore dirty ripped clothes to school every day. She felt sorry for the girl and often wondered where her parents were at. Keisha dropped the jump rope and ran over to the group of kids. "Leave her alone!", she yelled. They all turned to see who would become their next victim for interrupting them. When they noticed it was Keisha, they instantly calmed down. Keisha six older brothers were known as the neighborhood thugs who didn't mind shooting, stabbing, or killing someone over their baby sister regardless of their age. As the crowd started to disburse Star thanked Keisha for coming to her rescue. For the rest of the schoolyear the two girls stuck together like glue. Star loved spending weekends at Keisha house, enjoying the huge soul food dinners her mother cooked every Sunday. While Keisha house was small and in a semi-bad neighborhood, it was still far better than the rat and roach infested projects Star called home. Keisha's brothers were expert shop lifters and supplied half the neighborhood with everything from shoes, clothes, and household supplies for half off. They kept their baby sister in all the latest fits, making sure she never had to ask a man for anything. Keisha had so many clothes in her closet she would send Star home with huge garbage bags full of clothes every week. By the time the two reached high school they had become best friends.

"Come on Star!" "It will be fun!", Keisha begged! Star laid in her bed staring up at the chip paint on the ceiling, as she listened to Keshia on the other end of the phone. She was tired of Keisha always trying to hook her up with one of her boyfriend friends. It probably wouldn't be so bad if Keisha at least tried to hook Star up with guys on her man Roger level. Roger was the neighborhood dope boy who ran all the blocks. The day he saw Keisha and Star getting off the school bus, he approached them. "Can I join you ladies?", he asked. Keisha rolled her eyes when Star said, "Sure!". Star flirted and chatted with Roger while taking in his expensive clothing and jewelry while they walked to Keisha's house. Roger really wanted the quiet chocolate beauty but when Keisha showed him no interest he settled on Star. "Are you coming in Star?", Keisha asked, once they reached the front of her house. Star wanted some time alone with Roger, so she decided to continue her walk home. "I'm good girl, I have something I need to take care of!", Star said. Keisha side-eyed her friend before walking in the house. Once they were around the corner. Richard palmed Star round backside. "You are carrying a heavy load for a girl your age!" Star shyly smiled. She had indeed blossomed at a young age. By the time she was sixteen, Star had full hips, perky breasts and a nice round ass. Keisha was unaware that Star had slept with all her brothers the nights she stayed over at their house. She no longer had to wear Keisha hand me downs because Keisha brothers now kept her laced in all the latest gear. When Keisha would ask Star where she was getting all new clothes from, Star would lie and say she had an older boyfriend who wanted to remain a secret. Roger grabbed Star's waist from behind and grinded up against her. He led them in the opposite direction of Star's house. "Let's go chill at the park for a minute!", he said. When they reached the park, Roger sat on top of a picnic table and pulled Star between his legs. She tried to kiss him on the lip, but Roger tuned his head away. The whole hood knew how many dicks Star lips had been wrapped around, there was no way his lips were going to touch hers.

Star didn't let it bother her when Roger avoided her kiss. She knew how a lot of guys didn't believe in kissing unless it was with their main girl. "What's up, you trying to be my girl or what?", he asked. Star blushed. Every girl in the neighborhood wanted Roger and out of all the girls he could have picked, he chose her. She could see herself moving out of her roach infested apartment and into Roger plush four-bedroom home, if she played her cards right. Star bit down on her lip, "What I have to do?" Roger laughed on the inside. Star was younger and dumber then he originally thought. Roger reached down and pulled up the tight mini-skirt Star wore and was pleased to find she wasn't wearing any panties underneath. He unbuckled his pants while placing his hand on the top of Star head and lowering her to the ground. Star wasted no time as she started to suck and slurp Roger like her life depended on it. She didn't care that she was in a park, in the middle of the afternoon, out in the open, where anybody could see what she was doing. "Play with that pussy!", he barked. Star reached down and started touching herself. Roger smashed her head further down his rod, causing her to gag. The sight of her head bobbing and weaving in his lap made him grow harder. This bitch head was fire, he saw why she had the whole neighborhood going crazy. He pulled out as he came hitting Star in the face with his load. "Damn!", he said buckling his belt back up and lighting a cigarette. Star reached in her bookbag and grabbed a napkin, to clean off her face. "So, when do I get to see my new home?" Roger looked at her and let out a loud laugh! "You didn't believe me, did you?" "What do I look like turning the neighborhood hoe into a housewife?" "But I will pay you for a blow-job on a regular basis.", with that Roger walked off leaving Star speechless.

Star walked home in tears, humiliated. She promised herself she wouldn't tell anybody about what happened. The next day Star and Keisha walked past Roger and his boys while they whispered and laughed. Keisha leaned in and whispered to Star "What the fuck is all that about?" Star shrugged her shoulders as they kept walking. Roger jogged to catch up with them and pulled a tiny brown bear from his inside coat pocket. Star heart sped up and just as she reached for it, he handed the bear to Keisha. "Something chocolate for my chocolate! he said. Keisha laughed at his corniness. "I finally got a smile!", Roger said reaching for Keisha books to carry them as they continued walking. "I smile all the time, just with people I know", she teased. After begging and pleading for Keisha's number the entire walk home, she finally gave in. Star felt like crying but held it in. "How dare he", she fumed. "Carrying this bitch books and asking for her number in my face". Star stormed off, ignoring Keisha calling her name. "Fuck that bitch! she mumbled. When Star got near her apartment, a hard shove from behind caused her to go tumbling forward. Thankfully, she caught her balance just before she hit the ground. "Let's talk!", Roger said, dragging Star towards the side of her building. "If you mention what happened between me and you yesterday, I'll kill you!" Roger poked Star in the middle of her forehead with each word he spoke to emphasize his point. He had a reputation for making his problems "disappear", so Star *knew he meant every word he said. "So, I'm not good enough for you?', she cried. "Bitch, you sucked my dick on a park bench in broad daylight!" Star cringed at his cruel words. He turned up his nose, "I need a woman a little classier, like Keisha!", he chuckled. From that day on Star secretly hated Keisha and she rarely stayed over at Keisha's house anymore. She would rather endure her mother's abuse then seeing Keisha and Roger together happy.*

Star silently watched Keisha prance around her bedroom as she tried on her prom dress. The aqua teal dress was filled with beautiful beads from head to toe. Prom was less than a week away and Star had yet to purchase a prom dress. Her unfit, trifling mother had not saved one dime for the special occasion. Keisha offered to buy Star's dress for her, but she refused. Star was tired of being Keisha's charity case. Four of Keisha's brothers were locked up, eliminating them as her sponsors. The other two had become bored with Star and was on to something new. "What are you going to do about a dress for prom?", Keisha genuinely asked. Star stood from the bed while gathering her things. "I have a plan!" Star walked out of Keisha's room without bothering to say bye. Star scrolled through her contacts as she headed towards her building. She punched in her building number followed by one thousand dollars and pushed send. By the time she arrived home, Roger was already sitting outside her building. Star got in the car and slammed the door. She flipped through the money sitting in the cupholder before stuffing it in her bra. Roger cut the radio up and leaned his seat back. The thousand dollars Star charged him was well worth it for the hour of fire head he was about to get. Roger loved Keisha, but he was addicted to Star. Roger kept food in Star's and her crackhead mother refrigerator, brought Star new clothes and even paid back her mother drug debts in the streets. Roger knew he was wrong for creeping around with Keisha's best friend, but Keisha refused to give him oral sex, so he had to do what he had to do. "What one bitch won't do, the next one will", he reasoned! He thought they were being low-key but maybe not low-key enough. Roger was in total bliss as he guided Star head up and down his shaft, when a brick came flying through the back window. Roger pushed Star off him, grabbed his gun from under the seat and jumped out the car. His heart dropped when he saw Keisha standing there crying. "How could you?", she screamed. Roger knew it was nothing he could say as he looked down at his dick swinging from side to side still glistening with Star's spit. "You left this!", Keisha screamed, throwing Star's purse at her. Star had been so busy trying to run out and meet Roger, she had left her purse on Keisha's bed. "Guess you can't help every welfare case!" she laughed. Keisha words stung Star like a bee. Is that how Keisha had looked at her all these years, as a welfare case? The one person in the world she thought truly loved her was only pitying her all this time. Fuck her, and her fake love! Suddenly, Star didn't feel bad one bit for fucking Keisha's man. At least she had got something out of it! She made sure the money Roger had just given her was still tucked safely in her bra before heading in the house, happy that she would at least still be able to buy her prom dress. Star promised herself from that day on, money is all that mattered. A couple of months later, Star was off to college where she met Richard who picked up right where Roger left off.

Chapter 13

King and Mya settled into married life quickly. King was
happy to have a beautiful wife to come home to every day.
After spending so many years in the streets, he was finally
looking forward to settling down and starting his family.
King cruised down the Lodge Freeway bobbing his head to
the latest Rick Ross album. He was anxious to finish up his
regular routine stops, collecting money from his spots so he
could get back home. If felt good to have a woman who
wanted him but didn't need him. Mya's Business degree
had earned her a promotion as a top financial advisor with a
fortune 500 company, making over six figures a year. She
wasn't like a lot of these thots out here that was running
around looking for their next come up. King was proud of
his wife. He wasn't one of those insecure weak men who
felt intimidated by their wife success. He found Mya's
independency sexy. King pulled up to his spot-on Dexter.
He always made this his last stop of the night, because it
was his top money maker. He grabbed his pistol from under
his seat and tucked it safely in his waistband before exiting
the vehicle. King was a veteran in the streets and always
showed a lot of love to his soldiers. He lived firmly by the
rule, "the boss will always become a meal, when he leaves
his workers starving". King made sure every person on his
team was fed and fed well. However, he still watched his
back heavy because you never fully know what the next
person is capable of doing or thinking. King stepped onto
the porch and gave the two men sitting in chairs a dab
before heading into the house. Rico, his top lieutenant was
sitting on the couch with a cigarette dangling out his mouth
fully focused on the video game he was playing. King
reached down and picked up the heavy black duffel bag
sitting on the side of the couch. "Everything is in there, old
man!", Rico playfully said, never taking his eyes off the
television screen. King chuckled, giving Rico a playful

shove. "I Got Your Old Man!", he said. Rico had become like a son to King over the past two years, watching him work his way up from corner boy to overseeing two of King's main houses, not once coming up short in product or money. King made sure Rico had enough product to last him a few more days before heading out. He couldn't shake off the feeling that someone was watching him as he jumped in his car and pulled off. He brushed off the feeling, anxious to get home to Mya.

King stood in the doorway of the kitchen and admired his wife plump ass jiggling around under the thin silk nightgown she wore. Mya was so into what she was doing, she didn't hear King come in the front door. Mya turned the stove on low before placing the perfectly seasoned steaks in the oven. She was preparing King's favorite meal for dinner; smothered steak, mashed potatoes, buttered corn and homemade biscuits from scratch. Mya turned the volume up on the kitchen Bluetooth when one of her favorite songs came on. She sang along with Beyoncé, off-key and at the top of her lungs, as she admitting to being, "Dangerously in Love!". Just as Mya hit a high note, she felt strong arms grab her from behind, causing her to nearly drop the tray of dough she was kneading. "Good thing I didn't marry you for your singing", King laughed while placing light kisses on Mya's neck. Giggling and trying to wiggle out of King's grip she said, "Oh No, Mister!" "I just put the steaks in the oven, and I don't want them to burn being distracted by you!" King ignored Mya words as he slid his hands under her nightgown and began caressing her breast. Mya let out a soft moan as he fondled her breast. King turned Mya around, and gently placed her on the kitchen counter. Mya squirmed around in anticipation as King spread her legs open as far as they would go and dropped down to his knees. King could not get enough of Mya's sweet juices, if he could live off it, he would. He lightly blew on her lower lips, teasing her. King placed Mya legs on his shoulders before letting his tongue dive into her wetness. He flicked his tongue in and out of her like a snake. Right when he felt her about to go over the edge, he replaced his tongue with his fingers gently massaging her clit. Mya eyes rolled to the back of her head as King sent her body in a frenzy. "Oh My God Baby!", she cried out while gripping the countertop for support. Mya legs begin to shake uncontrollably, as her body rocked from a powerful orgasm. King made sure he caught every drop of her sweetness before lowering her legs from his shoulder. King stood up and dropped his jeans around his ankles. He wrapped Mya legs around his waist before sliding into her. He bit and sucked Mya's neck as he glided in and out of her. Mya body became paralyzed when King found her spot and beginning slowly grinding into it. A single tear rolled down her face as her second orgasm took over her body. All she could mutter was the words "I love you!". The feel of Mya juices trickling down his dick like a waterfall was all it took for King to grunt and release his seeds into her. Neither one of them moved right away relishing in the afterglow of their orgasms. They both jumped at the sudden sound of the smoke detector going off. "Shit!", Mya shrieked sliding off the counter onto wobbly legs. Mya grabbed a dish towel and snatched the pan of steaks out the oven while King opened a window to let some of the smoke out. King and Mya both laughed looking at the burnt steaks stuck to the bottom of the pan. "Pizza and Movies?", they both said at the same time.

Chapter 14

"Who the fuck is blowing up your phone up like that?",
Mya snapped, covering her head with a pillow. For the past
thirty minutes King phone had been ringing back to back.
Normally he would never ignore his phone but the all-night
sex session him and Mya had after watching a movie went
well into the night. King rolled over and grabbed the
ringing phone off the nightstand. "Yo!", he barked into the
phone. "Nigga get down to the meeting place NOW!", Don
yelled into the phone. King jumped out of bed and begin to
throw on his clothes. Mya sat up alarmed. "Baby what's
wrong?" King didn't want to worry his wife until he knew
exactly what was going on. By the tone of Don's voice, he
knew it was something serious. "Go back to bed baby", he
said giving Mya a quick kiss on the forehand. "Just some
business I need to take care of really quick!" "I'll be back
in a minute!". King grabbed his phone and keys off the
dresser and jogged out the room. Mya laid back in the bed
and said a prayer for her husband. She knew he was into
some illegal activities but with the investments he had
made over the years and her hefty income they both agreed
it was time for him to hand over his reign and get out the
game. Mya just hoped nothing had happened to stop them
from their plan.

Don and Rico were waiting inside King's office when he
arrived. He could tell from the look on their solemn face
that he wasn't going to like what he was about to hear. Don
slid the bottle of Hennessey he was sipping on across the
desk to King. King took a long swig before sitting the
bottle back down and leaning back in his chair. Don placed
a large manila envelope in front of King. The room was
dead silent as King dumped the contents of the envelope
onto his desk. His heart sank as he flipped through photo
after photo of him and Don going in and out of their
different trap houses. King instantly thought back to the

other day and the feeling he had that someone was watching him. Don gave King a minute to gather his thoughts before simply stating "We have a rat!" King and Don had taken extra precautions over the years to prevent something like this from happening. They had several police officers and even one district attorney on their payroll. What they didn't expect was to be blindsided by a federal investigation. King knew it was nothing the people on his payroll could do to intervene when the feds were involved. "How did this happen?", King wondered. As if reading his mind, Don said, "They have an informant who has been giving them inside information on our operation." King grimaced in anger. They took care of all their soldiers well making sure to keep their pockets swollen. They ran their operation like a corporation, going as far as handing out holiday bonuses to every member of their team just to show appreciation for their loyalty, only to turn around and be betrayed. King was insulted to say the least! "Get as much information from our police contacts as possible!", he barked. "We are shutting everything down immediately, until further notice!" King could see the look of worry on Rico's face. He knew the young man was responsible for taking care of his sick mother and two younger sisters. That was one of the reasons King had brought him on board. Rico reminded King a lot of himself when he was younger.

King walked over to his wall safe and punched in the combination. He took out three large stacks of money and handed them to Rico. "Here is fifty thousand to hold you over until we figure everything out bro". Rico fought back the tears that threatened to fall any moment from his eyes. For his entire life Rico had always made sure everyone around him was straight, it touched his heart for someone to care enough to make sure he was good for a change. King and Rico exchanged nods; no words were needed. After being in the game for all these years, just when he was ready to get out this bullshit happens. King knew time wasn't on his side. If the feds had pictures, their case was pretty much built, and it was just a matter of time before he and Don were picked up and indicted. King had to collect his money out the streets and flip the rest of the kilos in their possession as quick as possible. There was no telling how much money he would need for lawyers, or even worse for his books and Mya security if he had to do prison time. King wanted to tell Mya what was going on but decided against it. There was no need for them both to be stressed out and worried. He just prayed this would all blow over. King pulled in his driveway and sat in the car and smoked a blunt to get his thoughts together before heading in the house.

Chapter 15

Mya was sitting in the living room idly flipping through channels on the television when King walked into the house. She jumped into his arms and planted kisses all over his face. She had been worried sick about him from the moment King left the house that morning. Mya knew King was heavy in the streets and the dangers that came along with it. They shared a long embrace, each lost in their own thoughts. Mya wanted to ask a million questions but figured King would talk to her when he was ready. "I'll get dinner started!", she said, breaking their embrace. Mya seasoned a few pieces of chicken breast before placing them in a pan to simmer. After pouring some rice in the steamer, she poured herself a glass of wine and headed upstairs to take a quick shower. As Mya passed the family room, she heard King talking on the phone in a hushed tone. When he noticed her standing there, he told the person on the other end he would call them back later. Mya heart sank, for the first time in their relationship she wondered if her husband was cheating on her. "I'm about to take a quick shower, the food will be ready shortly!", Mya sadly said. She turned and walked out the room quickly before King could respond. Mya lathered and moisturized her body in King's favorite vanilla scent. She threw on a pair of red lace boy shorts, with the matching bra. If King was cheating, Mya wasn't going down without putting up a good fight for her marriage.

King sat on the couch staring off into space. Just looking at his beautiful wife knowing what he was facing broke his heart. After talking with his lawyer a few minutes ago, King learned things were far worse than he expected. The feds were investigating him for drug trafficking, money laundering and at least one murder. King had not got to where he was by being a saint. He demanded his respect in the streets, even if it resulted in murder. He had done so much, there was no way of telling which murder he could possibly be under investigation for. When he heard the shower cut off King headed to the kitchen to fix Mya's and his plate. "Thank you, baby!", Mya said as she entered the kitchen. King admired his wife curvy body in the lace bra and panties she was wearing. Normally he would be standing at full attention and ready to rip the thin material off his wife and devour her. But with everything going on his mind was distracted. King brushed past Mya and sat their plates down on the table. Mya fought back her tears as she grabbed them two bottled waters out the refrigerator. The two ate dinner in silence both lost in their own thoughts.

Chapter 16

When Star pulled into the circular driveway of Don's home her mouth dropped in surprise. She knew Don was living large, but she didn't expect to see the massive estate in front of her. There had to be at least ten different luxury cars lined up in the driveway. Star checked her reflection in the mirror before hopping out the car and heading to the door. Before she could knock an older black gentleman dressed in shirt, tie and slacks opened the door and greeted her. "Right this way ma'am", he said. Star looked around in amazement as she was led through a kitchen with marble countertops and floors. They stepped through a set of double French doors, out onto a two-story balcony overlooking Don's massive back yard. Don sat the newspaper down he was reading and stood to give Star a hug. She inhaled the scent of his Gucci cologne as she hugged him back. Over the last few months the two had spent a lot of time together normally in five-star hotel rooms. This was Star first time being invited to Don's home and she hoped this was a sign of them working towards becoming exclusive. Don was everything she desired in a man, handsome, rich, and charismatic. Star knew he entertained other women, so she made sure to put it on him every chance she got hoping it was enough to make the others disappear. "Hey Daddy!", she cooed. Don squeezed her ass through the sundress she wore. He grabbed her by the hand and led her into the house "Let me give you a tour!" They walked up a long spiral staircase and past several bedrooms the size of mini apartments. The master bedroom décor was masculine but elegant, in rich colors of gold and black with a king size California bed sitting in the middle of the room. After showing Star around the upper level, Don led her to the basement, which was equipped with a heated jacuzzi, home theatre, and game room. Star tingled all over just thinking about the extravagant house becoming her new home soon. She had come a long way from the ghetto projects she grew up in. Don grabbed Star around the waist and lightly kissed her on her neck. "Now its your turn for show and tell", he whispered in her ear. He gave Star ass a rough smack as she led the way back upstairs to the master suite.

Don palmed Star round ass as she bounced up and down on top of him. He leaned in and lightly bit her hard nipples causing her to cry out in ecstasy. Star threw her head back in pure bliss as an orgasm took over her body. Since sampling her goods on the yacht, Don was hooked on Star and stayed buried in her warmness on a regular basis. She was a super freak in the bedroom and would do anything to please him. Star could give the chic Super Head a run for her money with her certified head game. Don deep moans turned Star on and encouraged her to go harder. Taking advantage of the huge king size bed Star placed her legs in a full split position and began to slowly rotate her hips in a circular motion. "What the fuck!", Don yelled out when he felt Star walls grip him. Don gripped Star's waist and pushed further into her. She continued sliding up and down on his pole until she felt Don releasing his load inside of her. Star laid her head on Don chest and whispered, "I Love You!". Don gently sat Star up and starred into her eyes. For the first time he saw the insecurity of a little girl. Don didn't want to hurt Star, but he refused to lie to her either. It was better to be honest about how he felt then string her along, so he chose his words carefully. "I love how you make me feel", he said. Star heart sank at hearing those famous words. Don was just like everybody else, if he had access to what was between her legs, he was happy, and her feelings didn't matter. Out of all the men Star shared a bed with over the years not one had ever tried to make their situation permanent, or exclusive. She was nothing more than a replaceable piece of ass to each of them. Star forced a smile, as she slid off Don's lap and started to get dress. Star made sure she kept her back to Don as she put on her clothes so he wouldn't see the tears falling down her face. She didn't even bother to say bye, when she walked out the room.

Don knew Star wanted them to become exclusive but, in his heart, he knew that would never happen. Star reputation was too flawed in the streets for him to parade her around as his wifey. Don had yet to tell King he was fucking Star because he knew she wasn't going to be around long term anyway. In Don's line of business, he needed his woman to be an asset to him instead of a liability. He understood things could change in a blink of an eye and needed to know his woman would hold him down if necessary. Don and King had been best friends since they were knee high. They built an empire from the ground up. Don knew what came along with the drug game, so he was not surprised when one of the police officers they had on payroll called him and informed him that both King and he were under investigation by the feds. Don loved King like a brother and would not hesitate to go down for them both if he could.

Chapter 17

Mya stared down at the bright two pink lines floating across the white stick. She should have been ecstatic to be carrying her husband's child but instead she was filled with dread. Until recently King had never given her a reason not to trust him. King was barely home anymore and when he was, he was moody and distant. They went from having sex two or three times a day, to hardly at all. Mya didn't want to believe her husband was cheating within the first year of their marriage, but all the signs were pointing in that direction. She sat on the bathroom floor clutching the pregnancy test crying. Mya watched her mother struggle as a single parent her entire life. She didn't want to bring a child into the world under those same circumstances. Mya had just received a promotion on her job as head financial advisor and was proud of her accomplishment. She had worked hard for the position and doubted that she would be able to manage her overwhelming job responsibilities and being a single mother if her and King were to divorce. Mya was torn on what to do. She knew if King found out she was pregnant there was no way he would allow her to abort his child. Telling her mother was out of the question as well because Mya knew she wouldn't understand. Her mother had raised her alone with only a high school diploma that only qualified her for jobs making minimum wage. There was no way her mother would understand why Mya was even considering an abortion when she had a job making six figures and could easily afford to raise a child alone. Mya gathered herself off the floor and jumped into the shower. She needed some girl time with her best friend. Mya threw on a Pink jogging suit, brushed her hair up in a messy bun, applied a light coat of lip gloss to her lips and headed out the door.

Maury was just about to announce who the baby father was when Star doorbell rang. Annoyed, she hit pause on the television and stormed over to the door. Star hated company, especially unannounced company. She rarely entertained at home, always requiring rooms in at least five-star hotels for her rendezvous. Star yanked the door open and was surprised to see Mya standing on the other side. Her and Mya had not really spoken much over the last few months. That was fine with Star, between Richard, Don and a few of her other "sponsors", she didn't have much time left to fake being happy for her "friend". Mya didn't even bother to say hi, before brushing past Star into the house. Star rolled her eyes and closed the door. All she wanted to do was get back to the drama on Maury Povich, not deal with drama from her so called best friend. Star walked into the kitchen and found Mya opening a bottle of wine. She reached into the cabinet and pulled out two wine glasses and poured them both a glass. Mya figured since she was unsure about keeping the baby a few glasses of wine wouldn't hurt. Star sat quietly while she waited on Mya to disclose the reason for her unannounced visit. After taking a few sips of wine, Mya blurted out she was pregnant. Star almost chocked on the sip of wine she had just took. This bitch officially was living the all-American dream she silently fumed. Mya had a good job, a good husband, a big beautiful house and now a bastard ass child to secure her attachment to King for the rest of her life. Before Star could respond, Mya burst into tears. "I'm not keeping it", she sobbed. "I think King is cheating on me!" Star sat there stunned. King the "Knight in shining armor", was cheating! Star nearly jumped out of her seat with joy.

So, everything wasn't peaches and cream in Ms. Mya perfect little world. Star had to fight back her smile as she slid closer to Mya and rubbed her back as she cried. She couldn't be happier, this is what Star had been waiting on since the day she laid eyes on King, a chance to wiggle her way in with him. Star waited patiently as Mya sobs turned into sniffles. Star walked over to the refrigerator and grabbed out another bottle of wine. She popped the cork and poured them each another glass. As they drunk their second bottle of wine Mya filled Star in on King's sudden long hours in the streets, mysterious phone calls, and lack of sex drive. Star had dealt with just about every type of baller, drug dealer and street niggas there was, and on all different levels because of her gold-digging ways. As she took in everything Mya was saying, Star realized there could be several different reasons behind King sudden change in behavior and cheating was far down the list. If Star had to take a guess, she would say King's behavior had something more to do with a situation in the streets then in his home. A blind man could see how much King loved and adored Mya. Star doubted very seriously if he would jeopardize his marriage for just some random pussy out here. Mya was pretty, intelligent, and loyal, and most men especially of King status knew that was hard, if not impossible to find. If Star was a real friend, she would have expressed her true feelings to Mya but because she took joy in seeing Mya suffer, she kept her thoughts to herself. Instead she chose to feed into Mya's insecurities. "I agree with you girl, it definitely sound like that nigga is cheating!", Star said before taking another sip of wine. "You would be a fool to have his baby". "Your career is just now starting to take off and without King's support who knows how long it will take you to get back to work". "Look at everything your mother went through trying to raise you alone, do you really want to bring a baby in the world under those same circumstances?" Mya thought long and hard about everything Star was saying. King's sudden change of behavior all pointed to one sign; he was cheating. He had never kept a lock on his phone in the past and use to come home at a decent time every night. That all changed over the last couple of months. King kept his phone locked and, in his pocket, always. Where he would normally call her throughout the day just to check on her, she now barely heard from him during the day at all, not to mention the constant disappearing acts. After sitting in silence for a few minutes, Star asked Mya what she planned on doing. Mya shrugged her shoulders, "I don't know", she sadly said. I have a lot to think about.

Chapter 18

Mya rolled over and looked at the clock when she heard
King coming through the front door. It was three o'clock in
the morning and he was just getting home. King was
startled to see his wife sitting up in the bed when he walked
into the room. "Hey baby!", he tiredly said. When Mya
didn't respond King stopped getting undressed and looked
at his wife. "Are you cheating on me?", Mya boldly asked.
She refused to be a weak bitch who sat around and cried
while blaming herself for her man cheating ways. Mya
knew she was a bad bitch and if King didn't appreciate her,
she would have no problem leaving him and finding the
next man that would. King sat down on the side of the bed
and dropped his head in his hands. He wanted to confide in
his wife, but with the possibility of him being indicted any
day, the less she knew, the better it would be for her own
safety. If she was picked up and questioned, she couldn't
tell what she didn't know! "Baby you have to trust me!" "I
love you and would never do anything to hurt you!" Mya
cringed at his response. Those were the exact same words
her father told her mother for years, before leaving her for
his younger mistress. "Love doesn't hurt!", she said, before
laying her head back on her pillow. Mya was right King
thought! It was time he told his wife the truth. Heading to
the shower he turned and said, "I'll be gone for a couple of
days on business!" "I will tell you everything when I get
back!" King and Don were flying out to meet with their
connect Max, and pay off their tab. After long hours in the
street every day and cutting their prices in nearly half, they
were able to move the rest of the product they had. They
decided to lay low while they plotted out their next move.
King hired one of the city's top lawyers to represent them
and now all he could do was wait it out.

Mya picked up her cell phone and googled Planned
Parenthood website, when she heard King turn the shower

on. Her final decision was made. After Mya found the location closest to her, she answered some basic health questions and typed in all her information. In less than ten minutes her appointment for tomorrow morning was confirmed and she felt relieved. Mya sent Star a text message asking her for a ride to her appointment the following day. She heard the shower cut off just as Star replied with "I got you best friend", with the sad face emoji. Mya deleted the message and slid her phone back on the nightstand by the time King came out of the bathroom. As Mya laid there pretending to be asleep, Star words played back in her mind "I agree with you girl, it definitely sound like that nigga is cheating!" "You would be a fool to have his baby!"

The next morning Mya sat at the kitchen counter drinking a glass of tonic water fighting the urge to vomit as she anxiously waited for King to leave. She wasn't sure if she was experiencing morning sickness or her stomach was just jittery from what she was about to do. Mya was having second thoughts about getting the abortion. What if this destroyed any chance of her conceiving a child in the future. Mya wished this was all just a bad dream that she would wake up from any minute. King came down the stairs dressed in all black from head to toe. The short sleeve, Tom Ford button down shirt he wore showed off his well-toned arms, and the matching black jeans gave him a hood, yet professional look. The diamond K pendant that dangled from his Cuban link chain complimented his outfit well. "You look awfully nice to be heading out on business!", Mya smirked. King gave Mya the side eye, before grabbing an orange out the fruit basket on the counter and giving Mya a quick peck on the cheek. "Ill call you when I land". He casually said, before leaving out the door. Mya waited until King was gone for exactly ten minutes before jogging upstairs to throw on a pair of Nike leggings with the matching T shirt. She sent Star a quick text message letting her know she was on the way before she got cold feet and backed out.

"I'm not sure about this" Mya said. Her and Star had been sitting in Mya's car outside the clinic for the past ten minutes while Mya debated on if she would go through with the abortion. Star was beginning to get impatient. She had to meet Richard in a couple of hours to secure her money for her rent and car payment that was due in a few days. Don had been calling her, but she refused to answer. Star had embarrassed herself by telling him she loved him, only to find out he didn't feel the same way. At least with Richard Star knew what it was, a "pay to play" situation. No more, no less. Long as she kept her legs open, Richard kept her pockets full. Unlike Mya, she didn't have a husband who made sure all her bills were paid without a care in the world. "I tell you what!", Star said. "Call King and if he answers tell him your pregnant!" "If he doesn't answer, you probably know why, and you walk in that clinic knowing you made the right decision!" Star knew King and Don were on a business trip because she overheard Don on the phone the other day arranging their flight while she was at his house. No phones were allowed on their connect property so Star knew King would not be able to answer Mya's call. Mya glanced at the clock, seeing she only had two minutes left before her appointment time she picked up her cell phone and dialed King's number praying in her heart he answered. When King's voice mail picked up, she hung up. Mya tossed her phone in her oversized purse and made her way inside the clinic with the weight of the world on her shoulders. Star made sure to snap a few pictures of Mya walking into the clinic because she was sure they would come in handy later. Two hours later, Mya walked out of the clinic with an empty heart and an empty stomach. All she wanted to do was go home and hide from the world.

Chapter 19

King and Don were happy to be headed back home early.
After meeting with their connect and paying their tab, they
reassured him they had everything under control and
jumped on their private jet both anxious to get back home
and resolve the personal issues in their lives. King was
ready to make things right with his wife and Don missed
Star. He hadn't talked to her since the day she walked out
of his home and he missed her. Besides great sex, the two
had a good vibe. Don and Star could talk about anything for
hours. Unlike some of the polished, bougie women he
dated, Star could relate to Don on a hood level. By her
growing up in the projects, she understood the rules of the
streets. Star could enjoy an ocean front lobster dinner or
ribs from the run-down neighborhood soul food restaurant
as well. Don and Star enjoyed trips to The Detroit Institute
of Arts one weekend and Hip Hop and R&B concerts at
Chene Park the next. Star was well rounded and outside of
her manipulative ways she had the potential to be a good
person. Don saw something in Star the other day that he
had never saw before, her vulnerability. That gave him
hope that maybe she was capable of feeling emotions for
somebody other then herself. When King noticed Don deep
in thought he asked his boy was everything okay. Don
looked at his friend for a minute before asking. "Is it wrong
to judge someone for their blemished past?" King raised an
eyebrow at his friend, "Judge not, less you be judged!"
"We all have a past!" Don nodded his head in agreement.
Don and King had both done some things in their past that
he would not want to be judged for today. Everyone
deserved a second chance to prove themselves and he was
ready to give Star her chance by giving her the "wifey
title". When their jet landed the two gave each other fives
and agreed to meet at their lawyer's office tomorrow
morning anxious to see where their case stood.

King threw his overnight bag down in the foyer and rushed up the stairs to find his wife. He held two tickets to Hawaii in one hand and a small Tiffany box in the other. Their anniversary was in a couple of days and he wanted to take his wife on a romantic get away before things got chaotic. He flicked on the lights in their bedroom and found Mya buried under the covers. Rushing over to the bed he lightly shook her. "Baby are you okay?", he asked. Mya groggily set up, "What are you doing back so soon?", she asked. King could tell his wife was not feeling well by the pale look of her dark skin. When Mya reassured him, she was okay King handed her the plane tickets and the Tiffany box. "Baby I know I have been distant, but I love you." "I would never do anything to hurt you". "If I ever keep anything from you, it's to protect you". "You are my rib, there is no way I could live without you!" Mya eyes misted at King 'words. She looked at the tickets and saw they were for two weeks, and on the same Hawaii paradise resort she had told King about when they first met. "Baby these tickets say we leave in two days!" "How can I get ready for a two-week vacation in just two days, she whined?" King kissed his wife lips, "All you need to bring is yourself!" "We will go shopping when we get there!" "Now open your other gift!", he joked. Inside the Tiffany box was a diamond necklace with her and King's initials and their wedding date. Mya sobbed in her husband's arms. How could she have done something so cold and thoughtless to a man who was so thoughtful, caring and, generous. If King ever found out about her having an abortion, she was sure he would never forgive her. And their marriage would be over. That was one secret Mya would take to her grave.

King told Mya to relax while he went downstairs and fixed her some soup. After he poured the soup in a pot and cut it on low, King grabbed his phone to check his messages and voicemails. He realized that he hadn't powered his phone back on since leaving the connects estate earlier. While waiting on the phone to cut on King stirred Mya's soup making sure it didn't burn. He punched in his password and scanned through the large number of missed calls and messages. He noticed several messages from an unknown number. When he opened the first message his heart nearly jumped out of his chest. There was a picture of Mya walking into an abortion clinic with the words, "Guess she not so perfect after all", attached to the image. King took his fingers and enlarged the photo. That was definitely Mya in the photo, and he knew the picture was recent because she was wearing the Nike outfit that he had just purchased from the mall for her the other day. King turned the soup off and stormed up the stairs. There had to be some type of logical explanation for this. "The soup done already bae?"

Mya head was titled back on the pillow with her eyes closed. When King didn't respond Mya opened her eyes and looked in his direction. The look on his face froze her in fear. "Tell me you didn't abort our baby", he asked in a calm, flat tone. The calmness in King's voice, sent shivers down her spine. Mya wanted to say no but by the look on King's face she knew he already knew the truth, so it was no point in lying. "I can explain!", she whispered. King punched the wall, leaving a huge hole the size of his fist. "Yes, or fuckin No!", he screamed! "I thought you were cheating", she sobbed! "So instead of being a woman, a wife and coming to me you ran off and killed our child!"

King's words stung, because Mya knew he was right. "You more of a conniving bitch then Star!" "Guess birds of a feather really do flock together!", he laughed before storming out the house. King jumped in his car and headed towards his favorite bar with Star following closely behind. Star had been sitting on the corner of King and Mya's street for the past few hours patiently waiting on her chance to strike. Star knew it would only be a matter of time before

King saw the message she sent earlier, and she was prepared and ready.

Chapter 20

Star sat in the corner of the bar and watched King as he took shot after shot, lost in his own thoughts. The women in the bar were like vultures and could smell when a man wasn't happy at home. King was a hood legend and women had no shame making it known they were willing to play any position he allowed them too, just to be a part of his team. Star laughed to herself as King waved off woman after woman that approached him. It would take more than just a fat ass to get a man like King, Star knew because she had been waving hers in his face for over a year now and with no luck. After his tenth shot, the barmaid Maria cut off King's drinks. She was close friends with King's mother and had known King for his entire life. Maria refused to play a part in him having an accident on the way because he was drunk. "That's enough big guy!", she said, removing the empty shot glasses from in front of him. Marie knew something was bothering King because he wasn't his normal cheerful self but decided not to pry. Her main concern was him to make it home safely. Patting him on the hand, Marie told King to come back tomorrow and take care of his tab. She didn't want him pulling out a wad of money in the bar while he was tipsy. King stood up and kissed the older lady on the cheek. "I owe you!" He walked out of the bar and was thankful to feel the fresh air. He didn't realize how tipsy he was until he stood up. Making it to his car King dropped his keys while trying to unlock the door. A peep toe red bottom heel stepped on top of the keys as he bent down to pick them up. "You really shouldn't be driving in that condition", a voice said. King raised his head and came face to face with Star. He grunted in anger. "Move bitch!", he said giving Star a shove to remove her feet off his keys. "You have turned my wife into a lying hoe just like you", he yelled! Star laughed on the inside. So, her plan had worked after all. King almost fell over when he bent down again to pick up his keys. "I'm not letting you drive like this!", Star said snatching the keys off the ground before King could reach them. Hitting unlock on King's car doors, Star slid into the driver's seat. "Either get in or call a uber!", she told him while starting up the car. King already had a pending case and he didn't need to add a DUI to his list of charges. He walked around the car and jumped in the passenger seat. Star laughed at him sitting there sulking like a kid. Before they could pull out the parking lot King had nodded off to sleep. Mya drove quietly making sure not to wake him before they reached their destination. Twenty minutes later, Mya pulled up to the Embassy Suites in Dearborn and dashed in. She was happy to see King still knocked out in the front seat when she returned. King opened his eyes to the fill of someone lightly shaking him. He blinked his eyes a few times trying to remember how he had left the bar. "After what you said about Mya back at the bar, I didn't think you wanted to be drove home!", Star innocently said while holding out the room car. She had to play her role perfectly if she wanted her plan to work. Snatching the key from her hand, King starting walking in the direction of the hotel room.

The numerous of shots King had taken at the bar was pressing against his bladder. He didn't have time to stand outside and argue with Star. He would have locked Star out the hotel room, but she still had his car keys. When King emerged from the bathroom Star was sitting on the bed, with her jacket and shoes off. "Isn't it about time you go fuck somebody for your next meal!", he spat while grabbing the remote control off the dresser and flopping down on the bed. "I'm about too!", she laughed. Standing up, Star slid the dress she was wearing over her head revealing her nude body underneath. The sight of her perky titties, wide hips, and plump ass had King instantly hard. King and Mya hadn't had sex in weeks. When Star saw the look of lust in his eyes she slowly walked over and stood in front of him. "You like what you see daddy?", she sexily said while caressing her nipples. Star leaned in and rubbed her perky titties across King's lips. The feel of King's lips against her skin sent an electric shock through her body causing her juices to run down her leg. King reached down in between Star legs and roughly rubbed. He slightly moaned at the feel of how wet she was. King didn't know if it was the alcohol or his anger towards Mya that didn't make him stop. Star lowered her body to her knees and rubbed Kings hardness through his jeans impressed with the size. She stuck her hands down in his jeans and lightly stroked him before pulling out his chocolate stick. Star mouth watered at the beautiful, thick, long piece in front of her. She spit on it twice before taking it fully in her mouth. Kings toes curled and mouth dropped wide open at the feel of Star's warm mouth. He watched in amazement as she switched from swallowing him whole, to licking up and down his shaft. King had been orally pleased by a lot of women, but none had ever given him a blow job this good. He now understood how she was able to pay all her high as bills so easy. King grabbed Star by the hair and pushed her down further on him. The sound of her gagging and chocking was turning him on. "Suck that dick!", he barked. When King felt himself about to cum, he didn't bother to tell Star. He held her head still as he came down her throat. Star happily swallowed all King's seeds. King pulled his still hard dick from Star's mouth and yanked her up roughly by her hair. Bending her over the bed, he forcefully rammed inside her. King was surprised at how tight she felt after all the men she had been with. Star came the minute King slid inside her. She tried to keep her balance as her body shook from her orgasm and King pumping in and out of her at the same time. She made her ass clap and jiggle while throwing it back. King loud grunts let Star know Mya wasn't putting it on him like she was. Star lost count of how many orgasms ripped through her bod from the pounding King was putting on her pussy. He snatched Star's head back while roughly slapping her on the ass. The sight of his large red hand prints on Star's huge yellow ass every time he smacked it, had him ready to cum again. King closed his eyes and got lost in Star's tightness and warmth. "Damn Mya!", he yelled out as he came. When he opened his eyes, King saw Star, not Mya looking back at him smiling. King looked down in disgust, watching his semen drip out of her. "Get Out!", he spat. Star laughed as she slipped her dress back on. She had just got what she wanted, and maybe more.

Chapter 21

Star hummed to herself on the way home in the back of the
cab. The feel of the sticky fluids between her legs made her
smile. After all this time she was finally able to lure King
between her legs. Like every other man he had fell under
her spell. King could try to deny her all he wanted but he
would come running back just as Richard and Don had. Her
pussy had magical powers that no one could resist. When
Star felt King slide inside her last night with no condom on,
she silently thanked God that she had stopped taking her
birth control pills months ago. Her original plan was to
trap Don, but it would be even better if King got caught in
her web. Star tipped the car driver to wait on her, as she
ran into CVS and printed off the photos, she had secretly
taken on her phone of her and King last night. She placed
the photos in a stamped envelope, addressed them to Mya,
and dropped it in the overnight mailbox. Once Mya saw
those pictures, they would crush her poor little world and
send King right into her arms. When the cab finally pulled
up in front of Star's house, she threw the driver a couple of
dollars before jumping out the car. As she approached her
front door Star noticed a huge bouquet of flowers with a
note attached sitting on her front porch. Star picked up the
bouquet and walked into the house. Placing the flowers on
the table she ripped open the card that read, "I love you
too!" Tears fell down Star's face as she read the note
repeatedly. She knew it was from Don because he was the
only man, she had ever told she loved in her life. Star
squealed in delight as she ran and jumped in the shower.
She was finally getting the wifey title that she yearned for
after all these years. After drying herself off, Star grabbed
a few of the roses out the bouquet and laid across her bed,
placing the flowers on her naked body. After snapping a
few pictures, she sent them to Don with one word,
"Wifey"! Just as she was about to text Mya and tell her the

good news her heart dropped. "Oh My God what I have done!"

King woke up the next morning with a pounding headache. Sitting up, he winced as images of the night before invaded his mind. He couldn't believe he really had stuck his dick in Star and worse than that, he enjoyed it. He felt himself rising under the sheets remembering how good her walls felt wrapped around his thick pole. Maybe he had made the wrong choice by picking Mya over Star after all. King laughed at his own thoughts, he knew Star was nothing more than a jump off. Even with what she had done King loved Mya and had to take some of the blame for what happened. Had he just been honest with her in the first place Mya would not have assumed he was cheating. Sleeping with Star last night was a mistake and made him just as wrong as Mya. The question now was, could they get past everything that had happened. King threw on his clothes and headed home. He needed to take a quick shower and meet Don at their lawyer's office.

Mya was nowhere to be found when King arrived home. After taking a quick shower, he threw on a Ralph Lauren jogging suit and dashed down the stairs. Running in the kitchen to grab a smoothie King saw Mya had left him a note on the refrigerator.

To My King,

Words can't express how sorry I am about what I did. All you have ever asked of me is to be honest and loyal to you, and I failed. I'm going to stay the night at my mother's house to give us a little space. I will be home first thing in the morning to start packing for our trip. Hopefully to rekindle our love.

King smiled reading the note. He decided if they were going to start fresh, he had to reveal his dirty secret too. Tossing the note on the table King headed out in hopes of getting some good news from his lawyer. Don and their lawyer Richard were already reviewing the case when King stepped into the office. "Sorry I'm late guys!", he said.

King stared at Richard for a few minutes trying to remember where he knew him from. "It will come back to me", he thought before grabbing a seat. Over the next two hours Don, King and Richard went over the Feds potential case against them. "Maybe it is not as bad as we think!", Don said while pulling his phone out to check his messages. He smiled as he opened the message from Star. She was laid across her bed naked and covered in the flowers he left on her porch that morning. "If I didn't know better, I would think you were in love my nigga!", King teased laughing at Don blushing at his phone. Don quickly typed in, "See you soon wifey!" and sent the message before sitting his phone on Richard's desk to put on his jacket. "I guess now is a good time to tell you!" "I am in love bro, with Star!" "Star!", King yelled. Don hoped King would understand but he was going to make Star his wifey whether King understood or not! "Man, I know how you feel about her, but I'm telling you, I think she has changed!", Don said. King dropped his head. Less than twenty-fours ago, he had his dick touching the back of the woman his best friend loved throat plus she was also his wife's best-friend. King had fucked up royally. Feeling Richards eyes on them, Don asked King to step into the hallway so they could finish their conversation in private. Richard stood there in silence as the men excited the room.

Was it possible that Don was talking about his Star? Noticing Don had left his phone on the desk Richard quickly picked it up and breathed a sigh of relief that the phone was not locked. Hitting a few buttons, he went to the last message in Don's phone. His body shook in anger, as a picture of Star's naked body came across the screen. Now he understood why Star had been ignoring his calls and request to see her lately. "That ungrateful bitch!", he fumed. After all he had done for her, paid her rent, brought her expensive jewelry, even putting her gold-digging ass through college because her crackhead mother couldn't afford her tuition. For her to just up and leave him for a low life drug dealer. Richard let out a sinister laugh, exiting out the message and placing Don's phone back on the desk.

"Idiots!", he murmured. Don and King didn't even remember he was Star's date to King's weddings. True enough Richard had been so busy keeping Star's legs behind her head most of the time on the yacht that they didn't come out of their suite much to socialize but the men had cross paths at least once. How can you call yourself a street nigga and can't even remember a person's face? No one knew how dangerous Richard could be, but it was time he showed everybody who they were really fucking with.

Chapter 22

After a long day, King wanted to do nothing more than go home and climb into bed. He decided to fix himself a sandwich and watch a little ESPN while he ate. After eating, King stripped down to his boxers and jumped into bed, pulling the covers fully over his head. He would deal with everything going on tomorrow, right now he just needed a good night of sleep. The sudden feel of heavy pressure on his chest awoke King from his sleep. His eyes popped wide open at the sight of his wife, straddled across his body, holding a gun to the middle of his forehand. Baby Wait!", King screamed. He tried not to make any sudden moves to startle his wife and cause her to accidently pull the trigger on the gun she was holding to the middle of his forehead. "I trusted you!", Mya sobbed, lightly brushing the tip of the gun against King's face. King could see the hurt, anger, and betrayal in his wife eyes. Looking back, King wished he would have just been honest and upfront with his wife months ago. Mya laughed, "Imagine my surprise when I got home this morning to find this in the mailbox!", she said, while hitting King across the face with a stack of pictures. King looked down when a few of the photos fell from Mya's hand, and landed on the bed. His mouth opened in shock, "That devious bitch!", he thought. In the photos, King's head was thrown back in pleasure, which explains how he didn't see the tramp taking the pictures. She had planned this all along. How had he let that sneaky bitch manipulate him into hurting the only woman he truly loved. Mya was his soulmate, his gift from God. "Mya, I Love you baby", he gently said. Mya sat quietly as she looked down and stared into her husband eyes. How had they got to this point? Just one year ago, they were saying "I Do!", in front of their family and friends during a gorgeous wedding ceremony. The man she gave her virginity too, the man she vowed to love for better or for worse. King and Mya were supposed to be on a flight headed to Hawaii in just a few hours to celebrate their one-year anniversary. But that would never happen now. There would be no celebrations, this year, or any other year for that matter. "If you really loved me, you wouldn't have put your dick in that nasty bitch!", she screamed, just before pulling the trigger on the gun, filling the room with nothing but silence.

To Be Continued.....

Made in the USA
Columbia, SC
31 July 2024

39783227R00052